ISMITA TANDON DHANKHER is 'A Lesser Known Poet'. Her poem, 'I Am Beautiful', won a prize in the Yahoo-Dove Indibloggers contest. She's also the author of the romantic thriller *Love on the Rocks*, released in 2011.

Ismita went to Sophia College, Ajmer, where she studied economics, history and sociology. After acquiring an MBA and a brief stint in the foreign exchange division of Thomas Cook, Mumbai, she took up poetry and prose wholeheartedly.

She's currently working on *The Song of the Sufi Masroof*, a book of photographs and poems. Ismita blogs at www.lesserknownpoet.com.

JACOB HILLS

Ismita Tandon Dhankher

HarperCollins *Publishers* India

First published in India by
HarperCollins *Publishers* in 2013

Building 10, Tower A, 4th Floor, DLF Cyber City, Phase II,
Gurugram Haryana – 122002, India
www.harpercollins.co.in

2 4 6 8 10 9 7 5 3

P-ISBN: 978-93-5029-649-3
E-ISBN: 978-93-5029-650-9

Typeset in 11/14 Adobe Jenson Pro at
SURYA

Printed and bound at
MicroPrints India, New Delhi

Note

There are countless nameless, faceless soldiers defending our borders, fighting the insurgents and maintaining peace. The pride a solider feels in laying down his life to safeguard his countrymen is beyond commendation. My father served the Indian Army for thirty-six long years and they were the most rewarding years of his life. Not many know that this unique organization has an excellent support system that looks after the families of its officers, both retired and deceased. My mother has experienced it first-hand ever since my father passed away. I have high regard for this institution and I am proud to be an army daughter.

Jacob Hills is a fictional account of the 1980s, when Indian society was truly repressive, the mingling of men and women openly seen as an aberration. Though the country had been independent for over three decades, the British Raj had left a powerful mark, evident in the hierarchical setting of the erstwhile British Army. The aristocratic drink-and-party culture was kept alive by select Indian officers and their wives. That is the background for this novel. The high moral tone that was the reaction of our society to the modernity it saw impinging on it is reflected in the tone of the protagonists here.

The book is not about a particular organization, but about people and the choices they make.

A life without love
Is like a park without children,
Bereft of laughter, of innocence ...
Like a temple without God,
A book without a reader,
A man without a woman,
Yet, many a senseless life is spent,
Craving the pleasures of the flesh ...

Prologue

The weather is changing. The leaves, so green just yesterday, are beginning to dry up. The days are becoming warm and the evenings sultry; summer is in the air, and I feel like I am drying up too. I want to run away, but my own shadow frightens me.

I did run away once, but that was a long time ago.

I ran from home to be with him, and then from him, exhausted in mind and spirit, I ran deep within. But this time I must go further, someplace my own voice can't reach me.

I may have brought it up before, I don't really remember … Like most people, I tend to repeat things that have left a mark on me over the years. My earliest memory of being really sad is from when I was six or seven. We stayed in a two-room house – my father was yet to be rich and famous.

We had a beautiful garden with a row of blue roses. Our neighbours had two ferocious-looking Dobermanns, Bozo and Bullet, ugly dogs with snipped tails. The first time I saw the two mate, I was terrified and I called out loudly to my mother.

'Bozo and Bullet are fighting! Bullet is bleeding!'

She came out and dragged me in.

'Bullet is crying! We have to get Bozo off her!'

I was asked to shut up and no real explanation was

offered except, 'They are playing.' But Bozo seemed so violent when they played. What kind of a game was this, where one hurt and the other kept hurting? I never went near Bozo and Bullet after that. I only watched from the window, even when they ate the carrots my mother left in the sun to dry for the pickle.

I couldn't have known then that someday I would live with a Bozo who didn't understand the word 'no'.

Then there is this other memory from around the same time, of a fight I had with my elder brother. We landed mean punches and kicks on each other, and he took the white plastic hairband off my head and broke it into two. It was one of the few pretty things I had, and it now lay broken at my feet. I looked at it and thought that no matter how hard I hit back at him, the hairband could never be mended; it would remain broken.

I cried for hours; after a point I didn't even know why. It was as if I had suffered a great loss. I don't know if six year olds can feel that kind of sadness, but I remember crying about something much more than my hairband.

I don't know the why or how, but often I feel like I have lost something vital, so vital that I feel the life force trickle out.

I look at the bruises again. They are turning purple. The old ones have only just begun to heal. One would think that by now my pain threshold would have increased, but no such luck. I howl every time he touches me, like an animal being gutted alive.

In the early years of our marriage, he pretended to be caring, at least outside the bedroom. I don't remember exactly when he stopped throwing those morsels of affection my way, but the memory of him hitting me for the very first time stands out distinctly.

The plants in the garden needed to be watered, so I carried a small bucket from the kitchen instead of waiting for the batman to do it.

When an officer joins the army, a soldier is assigned to look after the young lieutenant sahib as his buddy. The buddy was called a batman, and it was his duty to fix the officer's uniform and polish his shoes, since the sahib had other, more important things to do. Once the memsahib came, it was understood that the batman would take orders from her as well.

This did not bother anyone – not the batmen, and certainly not the officers or their wives. It was their birthright. But it troubled me to see able-bodied men do household chores such as gardening, boiling rice, walking the dog and starching the memsahib's cotton saris.

But who was I to question systems that had been around since the time of the British, and would probably continue for decades to come?

My husband too leant heavily on the batman and treated him like an ordinary servant.

He came out to where I was watering the plants and said, 'We have got people for that; you come inside and do what a wife is supposed to do – bear children.'

That was the Sunday afternoon gin-and-soda talking.

I had scoffed at my father when he had advised me against marrying beneath our class. What is a little class and education that it can keep lovers apart?

He spoke again in a belligerent tone and kicked the bucket out of my hand.

'You are the lady of the house; at least act like one in front of the batman!'

In those days I had a voice. 'I would, had I married a real officer!'

I lost it very quickly though, when he caught me by the hair, dragged me inside the house and threw me on the bed. My frail body was no match for his strength. He pinned me down and a tight slap across the face left me speechless.

I lay there, tracing in my mind the trajectory of the teardrop that rolled out of the corner of my eye. Any minute now, I thought, he will apologize. He surprised me instead by unbuttoning my blouse. From that moment on, numbness had a new name: sex. The woman who can't be tamed by force can be tamed by sex. It's the ultimate violation of a woman's psyche; it shames her into silence.

That was my first lesson in being an obedient wife. I learnt many more over the years, and the most important one was that no one was going to save me, least of all I, myself.

And with that, surrender came easily.

It became a routine. He would rough me up, get aroused

and take without giving or caring. Ours was a love marriage; I had loved him enough to elope with him. I was fooled by his slick manner, chivalry and the dashing figure he cut in a uniform, the last of which lent him the class that his birth couldn't. He treated his men shabbily and his women worse.

I was unable to see through the fresh coat of paint that hid the ugly seepage of his upbringing. Many monsoons followed and the seepage eventually spread from him to me. From one, we became two ugly people, living our lives behind the facade of a respectable, happily married couple.

Time was slow in passing and tossed me about like a small boat caught in a storm. There were many such nights and I eventually lost count.

I am little more than a corpse now, after spending day and night at his beck and call.

Of late, the nights are gentler on me – he likes them young.

I was horrified when I heard that the seven-year-old daughter of a fellow officer had complained to her mother that my dear husband had pushed his tongue down her throat. Word had spread and he was forbidden from the living rooms of many, especially those with little girls.

I don't miss the socializing and no one misses me. The last couple of years haven't been kind to me. I walk down the road and nobody notices I am there.

I speak to someone and they don't hear what I say. I look in the mirror and I don't like what I see. Oh, so much ugliness; I tremble at the sight of my own reflection.

No one suspects that I am little more than a sex object in the confines of our home, definitely not the people who used to come home for elaborate dinners and lunches. There are no tell-tale signs.

He's clever that way; he never touches my face. It only gets ugly as you go lower. The cigarette burns on the inside of my thighs are not a pretty sight. He often misses the ashtray in his hurry to fill me.

He has done it again, his favourite game, to kiss and burn.

The Betadine stings, as I use the swab to clean the bruise. I better be careful when I visit the Medical Inspection (MI) room next – it's the second bottle of Betadine that I have taken this month.

The lies slip out quite easily. 'Oh, it's for the children. My younger one is always falling and hurting himself.'

There are no children, despite the routine nightly romps. Perhaps, this is his way of punishing me for not bearing him children.

A life of purgatory is what he has chosen for me. With his name and the comforts that come with his rank, some would say, my station in life is quite enhanced.

'It would be ridiculous to complain about a few nasty bruises, woman,' he says.

A respectable woman, I live in this fairytale palace with neatly cut grass, a white fence around the garden, servants to order around and fine gentry to mingle with.

Sadly, mingling with the finest doesn't make him one. He walks and talks like them, does all the things befitting an officer, and hides his complexes behind the impressive olive uniform. No one can tell that he's a sadist.

I don't complain, except in my head, where I wish his black soul would burn in the fire of hell.

I bide my time, till in a fit of rage he hurts me, or better still, kills me.

I am sure the doctors at the Military Hospital would be interested in finding out how his wife acquired so many burn marks down there.

But he will not kill me. He's a coward, and a coward always stabs in the back.

War College

Jacob Hills

The year was 1985. My husband sat across from me in the first-class compartment of the Himachal Express. George, clad in a military uniform, looked out of the window, hoping to catch a glimpse of the sun. The snow-capped mountains, unaffected by the biting cold and the absence of the radiant sun, stood in stoic silence, distant as my dear husband.

My attempts to strike a conversation with him met with faint 'hmms'. He's not much of a talker. After a while, I gave up and turned my attention to the enchanting scenery. I was getting to know his moods. He was a little apprehensive – a new place and new people seemed to make him edgy. I had come to the conclusion that he was bit of a loner.

So much had happened since our wedding last July. A

sigh escaped my lips and fogged the windowpane. It was noon; yet the air was thick with mist, a translucent white sheet conjuring shapes and forms for the wary traveller.

My toes were curling even though I was bundled in a beige fur coat; the tweed bell-bottoms were not of much use either. The cold was keeping me from truly admiring the landscape. I tried to see what George found so engaging outside. According to my mother, regardless of the Indian blood running in his veins, he had very English tastes.

Maybe that's what prompted my mother, Catherine, to accept George's proposal for me, after rejecting a dozen suitors. My grandfather, Riley, had come to India in the 1850s as a gangly youth in his twenties. He was a part of the team that laid India's first railway line from Howrah in Calcutta to Raniganj in Bihar. He married and brought his family to India. My mother was the youngest of five children, and married my father, an Indian engineer from the railways, when the freedom movement was at its peak.

There was great unrest in the country then. Her parents insisted that she join them on the vessel that was sailing to Southampton, but Catherine chose to stay. I was born a decade later in a free country. They named me Eva.

An Anglo-Indian heritage is not easy to lug around, the dislike for the white race still runs deep. But they are still in awe of fair skin and blue eyes. India has been independent for thirty-seven years, but I still get stared at. My mother used to say, 'It's my deep blue eyes that fascinate them.' She's old school, a bit of a racist.

George would say to me, 'If it weren't for your eyes, you could pass for an Indian.'

'I am an Indian!' I would flare up, and he would give me one of his more tolerant smiles.

He hadn't smiled since the accident. The limp was less pronounced now, but there were bitter reminders every day that things weren't as they used to be. He couldn't run or play squash. He had to rely on me for small things, such as tying his shoelaces.

I loved that time in the morning when George was getting ready to leave for office.

He polished his rank badges with Brasso. The rank badges of a major, comprising the lion capital of Ashoka with the motto 'Satyameva Jayate', are worn on his epaulettes. He rubbed the badges with a cotton cloth very diligently till the oxalic acid in the Brasso broke down the tarnish and brought out the shine.

I found it very endearing, the way his head tilted slightly as he inspected the brass plates after he had rubbed them vigorously. He has always been a man who does the smallest things to perfection and takes pride in them.

Next were the big black DMS boots, which he polished till he could see his reflection in them. He lived by the motto that happiness lay in small things that most people don't care about. He probably had no clue that these small gestures reminded me every day why I loved him so much.

In the mornings, I sipped my cup of tea and watched him

hop about pulling his uniform off the hanger, a fresh pair of socks and vest in hand, as he mumbled, 'I am running late'.

In most army homes, the batman got the sahib's uniform ready, but not in ours. George took pride in getting his uniform ready himself. In the beginning, I didn't think much of it, but with time, I had come to appreciate these small things that set George apart from the rest.

At the moment, George was grouchy because of his posting as an instructor at the War College in Jacob Hills. It was a profile coveted by most, but no, not by my George; he didn't want the cushy job of teaching in a classroom.

He asked me to look outside and I had my first glimpse of Jacob Hills. It was built like an old fortress – guarded by a high boundary wall with bright red rhododendrons fluttering like flags in the wind.

The surrounding forest lent a mystical element to the place and the chatter of the great barbet echoed in the background.

A giant clock tower dwarfed the stone turrets that George told me was Jacob Hall, which was built in the middle of the forest to permit greater access to the Bengal Tiger. This was a favourite hunting ground of the British before Independence. Jacob Hall still contained several tiger trophies.

Jacob Hills assumed importance when the armament factory was set up here in 1900 and the inflow of British officers increased considerably. The infrastructure necessary to sustain them and their families was put in place and Jacob Hills became a self-contained unit. After the 1971 Indo-Pak war, the Indian Army converted Jacob Hills into a training establishment, since there were no longer any tigers to be hunted or protected.

The imposing structure known as Jacob Hall now served as the War College, a training ground for nearly three hundred senior and junior officers pursuing courses in advanced weaponry in the Skills at Arms Wing; commando training in the Tactical Wing; technical training in the Communications Wing and espionage in the Physical and Intelligence Training Wing (PIT).

The trend predicted by the defence strategists required that the army train its officers, not only in combat, but also in espionage – and that is how PIT was set up.

Thirty of the sharpest Young Officers (YOs) from the various arms were handpicked to be trained for sensitive tasks. They were sent on a nine-month long rigorous programme to Jacob Hall, where they underwent intensive mental and physical training.

Depending on their final grades, the YOs were posted to different locations all over the world. The crème de la crème was sent to the developed nations as military attachés, while the others were posted to the Third World countries of Africa and South East Asia. The ones at the bottom of the course were sent to the border areas of J&K and Bangladesh.

It was an elitist course that would eventually catapult a few to the highest echelons of power and prestige, while the others would crawl slowly towards their retirement. Many of India's top-ranking officers were PIT pass outs, and it set them apart from the regular soldiers in the army.

I knew all this because my father-in-law, retired Lt. General Chandy, and George discussed it at length. George had been adamant about refusing the posting and had even accused his father of using his connections to secure his crippled son a place at Jacob Hills.

'Papa, you know damn well that I didn't get enough alphas in my courses to make it as an instructor. I appreciate your help, but I don't need it,' George had said to his father.

But Papa was sure this new posting was what he needed for his leg to heal completely – a low-pressure job in a scenic location. Within a year, he would be a new man.

I hoped so too.

'And you, Eva, how would you fare in this new life?' Papa had asked.

'Fairly well, I suppose.'

A porter peeped in as the train came to a halt. George dismissed him, saying there wasn't much luggage. I restrained myself and remained silent. The doctor had asked him not to put any pressure on his femoral bone. He took one of the bags and got off, asking me not to bother with the rest of the luggage.

He walked about to stretch his leg, and I looked around the station. There were a few stray benches here and there, but only very few people around. Not even a chaiwala in sight. A frail dog shivered from the cold and changed his position. The station master stood yawning, a green flag in his hand.

I noticed a tall Sardar, sporting a scarf around his neck and a stylish black turban, walk our way. He was followed by two soldiers, dressed in combats and black berets.

He strode up to George and slapped him on the back. George was stretching his leg and almost lost his balance. His cheeks flushed red as the handsome Sardar gave him a hand. I would have rushed to his side, but he would have resented that, especially in front of a fellow officer. I held my breath.

'Georgy, porgy, pudding and pie, kissed the girls and made them fucking cry!' the Sardar said in a loud voice and laughed.

George looked up at the fellow and broke into a smile. They back-slapped each other and hugged.

Interesting, I must ask George about the nursery rhyme – though he had admitted on several occasions that, before meeting me, he was quite popular with the ladies.

Going by the nursery rhyme, he hadn't been exaggerating.

In time, the men figured that it was only right that I am not kept waiting.

'My wife Eva; Eva, this is a very dear friend and a course mate of mine, Lieutenant Colonel Gary Randhawa.'

'Welcome to Jacob Hills, Ma'am. Your beauty takes away some of the austerity of this man. I have known him since our academy days; he's a difficult chap to live with.'

'I manage, Colonel.'

George took my hand and put it in the crook of his arm. We walked towards the exit, the Johnnies followed with our luggage and the porters looked on.

A jeep waited for us outside – from it, two more Johnnies jumped out when they saw us approaching. They saluted and said 'Jai Hind, saab' in unison.

A similar greeting minus the salute was made to me. My reply startled them a little. I could speak Hindustani fluently, not a trace of the British lineage that marked my features.

The drive to Jacob Hills took us through a steep terrain. In many places, we saw soldiers on horseback disappearing into the dangerously craggy hill range. Gary mentioned that it was considered unsafe to enter the jungle; the villagers had reported leopard sightings quite often.

I could see a cluster of thatched roofs in the distance and herds of cows and sheep that grazed and wandered in all directions. It was very refreshing after the city life I led in Calcutta. I felt childishly excited when I spotted a deer on the side of the road, waiting patiently for our vehicle to pass.

'How wonderful! He is not at all scared that we'll harm him!'

'They are not threatened by people after the government

passed the Wildlife Protection Act in 1972. Animals are hardly ever hunted in these parts,' Gary said.

I saw a blue bull grazing as we neared the establishment. I waved at it playfully and saw George rolling his eyes. I didn't care. I just felt so happy, as though we were on a jungle safari.

Abruptly, the terrain became steep. Although the jeep climbed steadily enough, the sudden increase in altitude made me feel dizzy.

'We're almost there,' said Gary reassuringly, noticing my pallor.

'Pam has cooked your favourite kadhai chicken. But you'll have some explaining to do on why we haven't heard from you since we were together in Bikaner last,' he said to George.

'You leave Pam to me,' said George, a smug look on his face.

'All yours, buddy.'

I had no idea that George had friends here. He had been so reluctant to come. Well, I was glad we came. Gary and his wife sounded like fun people. I had not had the faintest idea that they existed. George didn't share much. Or perhaps there hadn't been enough time.

We had been married only two months when George got injured. His convoy carrying food and medical supplies to the Mizo hill district was ambushed by the Mizoram National Army. A mine blast had blown up the truck in front of them and the impact had overthrown George's truck. Twenty soldiers were blown to death; there was nothing left of them to send home.

George's femoral bone was crushed under the wheel, but in spite of his injury, George had shown presence of mind and commandeered his men to safety. The troops retreated to the base camp without engaging fire and the lives of ten severely wounded soldiers were saved.

Later that night, the soldiers, as a follow-up to the ambush, torched the village in which they thought the attackers were seeking shelter. The hostiles were killed and captured, but many innocent women and children also died during the raid. The backlash was tremendous.

George suffered through all of that and was in the hospital for eight months. The multiple surgeries took a toll, as did the inquiry into the death of innocent villagers.

The scars of the mind were worse than the scars of the flesh, and he was given to prolonged periods of silence. Even now, he would wake up from his sleep screaming for his men to run for cover, or reminisce about collecting the bloodied body parts, trying to recognize who was who. There were young wives, little children and families back home who needed to see the bodies of their loved ones. Lying in that hospital bed, George became a different man – not the one I had married. Such close encounters with death can change one forever – for better or for worse. I prayed to the Virgin Mary to heal his scars.

We had already come far when the jeep stopped briefly at the barricade. Gary fished in his breast pocket and flashed an ID card that hung from a silver chain. The sentry noted the details of the vehicle and the personnel before allowing us to move further. After the barricade, the road became narrower.

The jeep coughed and sputtered along the way. There were moments when I thought the old girl would roll backwards, and we would all be tossed in the air and end up at the foot of the valley. None of that happened, though. She climbed up steadily, like a mountain goat.

Autumn had stripped the trees bare, but the red-white stripes painted around the tree trunks lent them a semblance of dignity. We crossed an old tank on display from the 1965 war and a Howitzer that was aimed at us.

Every building was encircled by a green hedge, kept in check by the brightly painted bricks. There were signboards everywhere, and men in khaki shorts sweated it out in the sun, carrying on maintenance work.

We crossed a signboard indicating family quarters. From this point on, the road became wide and snaked up a few levels of housing. At the bottom-most rung were independent bungalows with wonderful gardens, garden umbrellas and wrought-iron swings painted white.

As we climbed higher, the houses became blocks, each block comprising a set of four houses. On the third rung, we stopped in front of block number forty-nine. Gary pointed to a balcony from which hung baby clothes. We walked up the stairs and, before we could press the buzzer or take in the colourful nameplate, a pretty woman with long hair yanked the door open.

She squealed with delight when she saw George.

'Pam, motherhood has not affected you in the least. You look lovelier than ever!'

'Marriage hasn't changed you one bit, you charmer! Not even a new year's greeting in three years and here you are, married and all. Come on in!'

The introductions were made, and she went about serving us water. While I drank the water, I took the opportunity to inspect her. A flamboyant Sardarni, tall and buxom. Her light, coffee complexion was very cleverly made more striking by her beautifully carved, thick, arched eyebrows.

She wore an orange shirt tied at the waist over tight-fitting pants that hugged her shapely bottom. Jacob Hills was not a village after all; people did dress up in this part of the country.

Soon George asked me to help Pam in the kitchen.

Her house wasn't very neat and it had that baby smell – a combination of Farex and Johnson's baby powder. The baby, she said, was asleep.

'I'll lay the table?' I offered.

'No, just stay and chat.'

An awkward pause followed.

'So, do you play cards? We have a little group here you can join.'

'I never did develop a taste for playing cards.'

'Well, it gets a little dull out here. They are gone the whole day.'

'I am sure I'll find something to occupy myself with.'

'Oh, with your colouring that wouldn't be a problem,' she said, stirring the chicken.

What did she mean by that?

'Is there a school here?'

'Oh, yes, the army school, the only school. I never thought I would let my child study with the jawans' children, but it's only for a year, so it's all right.'

'Why? What's wrong with that?'

'They have no manners. Their noses run and their hair is full of lice. Very uncouth.'

This woman was beginning to remind me of my mother.

'I could teach at the army school,' I said.

'Sure, at least that way my child will learn a thing or two.'

Gary's voice came from the living room asking us to join them. Then George called out to Pam and she said, 'A minute, Georgy.'

George hated being called Georgy, but it did not seem to bother him today.

She started chopping coriander leaves and mumbled, 'The idiot forgot to cut coriander.'

The idiot was the batman, of course, memsahib's personal servant.

'We heard about the accident. What a terrible thing to happen to you, newly married and spending all that time in the hospital.'

'It was all right for me, but tough on George. He's not used to such long periods of inactivity.'

'Poor thing. He's such a virile man.'

God, this was one hell of an audacious woman! I was referring to a normal activity like being able to walk. I had heard many jokes about Sardars and their dimwittedness, but this woman here stole the cake.

The lunch turned out to be a bit too spicy for me but I could see George licking his fingers.

Great, my cooking had never inspired such passion in him. My cooking is subtle. George calls it bland.

Two hours later, we said our thank yous and goodbyes.

'You had a good time, darling?' George asked me in the car.

'Oh, yes, Georgy,' I answered, mimicking Pam.

He gave me that look.

'What? If your dear friends can call you such endearing names, why can't I?'

'Eva, they are nice people. You'll get to like them.'

'Ah, well, I hope I don't have to suffer through her company too often.'

'Darling, it's a small station and you'll be bumping into her every now and then. I suggest you learn to tolerate her, she has her pluses.'

'Like what, a big bottom?'

Grinning, he said, 'Eva, you mean little thing. Wait till we get home.'

Saryu

The Stepping Ladder

'Pull the damn thing down! Is that how you wear a sari, like a pair of goddamn high-waist trousers?'

He came and pulled the sari low – dangerously low – like some of the other women who draped the sari elegantly to display their curved waist and flat navel. I pulled the sari a little higher when he wasn't looking.

I adjusted the blouse as best as I could, the skimpy blouse tied in the front made me uncomfortable. It covered too little and showed too much of my non-existent cleavage. Vikram insisted that I get clothes stitched like those worn by the other wives. I had, but they didn't do much for my face or figure.

Vikram had thrown away the insipid browns and garish magentas that had come as my trousseau. He told me that if it hadn't been for my parents groveling for his hand, he would have married someone whose face didn't resemble that of a horse, and body, a bag of bones.

He, of course, never mentioned the large dowry, the car and the land he had readily accepted as a pay-off for my ugliness.

His folks belonged to the middle class in Patna and had survived on minuscule government salaries all their lives. As for Vikram, cracking the SSB in the seventies was tough and he made it in the third attempt. The proud parents bragged that their son was going to be a general sahib some day.

His rank as a captain commanded a certain price in the marriage market in Bihar, one my father had struggled to match. The wedding was a lavish affair and over a thousand baratis came, ate, drank, spoke ill as all baratis do, and left. The groom's parents were happy, but the groom felt cheated – a plain wife, without such accomplishments as grace and beauty is hardly an asset to an ambitious man in the army. And Vikram was highly ambitious.

His hunger got him to the rank of a major, but from there the road turned steep. The Annual Confidential Report (ACR), the equivalent of a report card for officers, depended on the whims and fancies of the senior officers and Vikram worked doubly hard to please them, yet his efforts were nowhere close to yielding fruitful results. His ACRs were mediocre and the next rank seemed like a distant dream.

Not one to give up so easily, my enterprising husband sat down one evening and narrated to me an interesting story of an ambitious couple.

I was more than eager to do anything to win my husband's regard and affection, and listened to him attentively.

He spoke of Pam, the wife of Lt. Col. Randhawa, who actively participated in the club, welfare and other activities, with the result that the couple had stayed on in Jacob Hills longer than any other instructor. Gary had also picked up the rank of a lieutenant colonel ahead of everyone in his batch and in the first shot.

I found Pam intimidating. She was articulate and beautiful and didn't much care what the other officer wives thought of her. It came as no surprise to me that Pam helped her husband in his work.

I longed to do so too, but God had neither been kind to me in the looks department, nor in speech. I could barely string a few sentences together in English.

I expressed my concern.

'You are nothing to look at, Saryu, but you aren't ugly either. If you took a little care of yourself, at least some pot-bellied colonel wouldn't mind having his ego stroked by you.'

It was much later that I realized it was not just the ego he expected me to stroke.

I was naive and lonely in a strange place, married to a man who had neither the time nor the inclination to be with me, unless I could in some way enhance his career prospects.

I took it up as a challenge. The ugly duckling couldn't

become a swan in a day or even a month, but I slowly learnt how to flatter his seniors – a smile here, a look there. It wasn't long before the colonel made his move and asked me for a dance at a ball. Vikram was happy to oblige.

'Your husband doesn't feed you too well.'

His sweaty hands squeezed my slim waist. I could only smile, Vikram was watching.

'Vikram tells me you are an excellent cook. I haven't tasted a home-cooked meal in ages. The food in the Mess is not worth feeding even stray dogs.'

The colonel's wife was in Delhi with the children who were giving their board exams, and that made the colonel a 'forced' bachelor. Such men usually had a field day eyeing others' wives; like most things in this world, this was fairly common too.

'So, when are you inviting me over, Mrs Singh?'

I hadn't answered him and that annoyed him a great deal. After the dance, he said to Vikram in front of me, 'Your wife is a little reluctant to invite me over for a meal.'

That night, Vikram was furious with me for insulting the colonel. He accused me of jeopardizing his career. Saturday was the day he had chosen to invite the colonel over for dinner.

I was in the kitchen the whole day preparing lamb, maharani dal, palak-paneer and missi roti. For dessert, there was phirni. I was happy with how everything tasted, confident that the guest would go back home a happy man.

I was laying the cutlery when Vikram came up to me and said, 'I am impressed with your culinary skills, but that's not all that needs to be on display tonight.'

'Yes, Vikram, please tell me what else needs to be done? I don't have any experience with these parties.'

'Dress nicely. The way to a man's heart may be through his stomach but his brain lies between his legs.'

I felt panic rise in me, but calmed myself. He was merely stating the obvious.

I chose printed chiffon in sea green, tied it really low, just above the pubic line, which was the trend. And if other wives could carry it off, why couldn't I? A backcombed bouffant looked nice. The false eyelashes with heavy eyeliner flicked at the end, made me look like the heroine's best friend in a movie, over made up but nothing to look at. I looked at my reflection in the mirror and said, 'You can do it, Saryu.'

Vikram barely glanced my way as he put his new alcohol collection on display.

'You bought all this for the colonel?

'Ambitious men don't depend on alcohol to take them places.'

No, they depend on their wives. I chased the thought out as soon as it arose.

The bell rang promptly at eight and in walked the honoured guest with a bunch of flowers from his garden, craftily put together by the batman, of course.

The colonel sipped his whisky and wiped his moustache with the back of his hand. Vikram bored him with anecdotes of the time he had spent at the Siachen glacier and how he had earned a commendation for it, a story I had heard several times.

I got up to serve them potato wedges. Usually, if people came over, Vikram expected the batman to serve and help out, but this evening he had been dismissed. I was to play the gracious hostess, both the men seemed happy with my performance so far.

Before dinner, Vikram insisted that the colonel and I chit-chat while he went and got ice cream. There were no ice cream parlours nearby. He would have to go further down to the village at the foot of Jacob Hills. The dreadful feeling returned.

We heard Vikram's Yezdi break the silence of the night and then fade into the distance. The colonel leapt up. He asked me if I would like to show him the rest of the house. What was there to show? There was just our bedroom and the study.

Still, not knowing what else to do, I showed him around. He murmured words like 'nice' and 'good' and stopped to examine the mirror in our bedroom. A photo frame on the dressing table had a picture of my parents; he asked me about them.

I said something but I wasn't really sure he was listening. There was this animal gleam in his eyes. He caught my wrist and said, 'Let's stop playing games for a moment and behave like adults.'

'I don't understand,' I said, shaking like a leaf.

'You have been leading me on and you don't understand?'

'Yes,' was my pathetic reply.

'Your husband did tell you to be nice to me, right?' He tugged one end of the knot that tied my blouse.

I snatched my hand back and ran to the study and locked it from the inside.

He didn't come after me. A minute later, the front door shut with a thud.

I sat there on the floor for a long time, crying, thinking inconsequential thoughts, such as how much food would be wasted. Vikram arrived an hour later. He banged on the door and asked me what happened. I came out and told him about the colonel's misbehaviour.

He started to laugh and said, 'Go look in the mirror. A man would find it difficult to get it up with you looking like this.'

The door closed and Vikram locked me out of our bedroom.

I went to the mirror and saw what Vikram had seen: the smudged eyeliner, the tired eyes and the undone bouffant. I looked ugly.

I remembered what my mother had said to me on my vidai, 'The only time you'll ever leave your husband's house is when he carries you on his shoulder to the funeral pyre.'

The husband, of course, could do no wrong. It was the wife's duty to keep the household together. I wish now I had paid more attention to what they taught in school.

I felt helpless. I couldn't go home; my parents had two more daughters to marry off. My return home would bring nothing but shame to them. I wasn't welcome there. They had done their duty, paid the dowry, and tied me to a man. I was on my own now. After weighing my options through a haze of tears, I finally realized that it was only a matter of time before I did exactly what the colonel had asked of me.

In that moment, I knew my life was not going to be like that of other women, looking after my home and children, waiting for my husband to come home.

If Vikram expected me to be on display, then that's how it was going to be. A man who loves his wife would never ask her to dress up for another man. And an unloved woman is a soft target – anyone can hit her, have her.

Stealth is Strength

The class is packed with thirty blank young faces. They have been here a month now, breaking their backs in the field: climbing ropes, crossing hurdles, trenches, running twenty miles a day, raising their fitness levels. They all look the same – lean and dog-hungry – half-asleep in the middle of the day due to exhaustion.

The YOs take the PIT motto, 'Stealth is Strength', very seriously and are always devising ways to miss their lectures and get proxy attendance. It was brought to my notice by Maj. Alex, one of the stuffy instructors, and I am here to sort them out.

'Behave like officers. You are not in the fucking academy anymore. Those of you who can't handle it, get the fuck out of my course. We don't need shammers here.'

Mid-way through my speech, many lose interest, only the front benchers, the sincere lot, listen in rapt attention. I know the majority of these men well. Just like their predecessors, they spend much of their time and money on wine and women, both of which are in plentiful supply. The girls' colleges in Shimla keep the YOs otherwise occupied.

Some things just won't change, and I see no reason why the class of 1985 is going to be any different.

I hand over the mike to the new chap, Maj. George Chandy. He limps to the podium in our newly built auditorium and introduces himself very formally.

I haven't really had a chance to speak with him yet. He arrived only yesterday. There is nothing outstanding about his service record that would land him a place in Jacob Hills, but for the son of a recently retired lieutenant general, that is hardly an issue.

In fact, these second-generation soldiers have a tendency to think of themselves as a cut above the rest. The army still suffers from a hangover of the British aristocracy, and if anyone's father, uncle or even a remote cousin is in the army, it's considered a big thing back home.

I must keep an eye on Maj. Chandy. We at PIT have a reputation to keep up. Only the very best are sent to train the best. Well, he certainly looks the part, we'll soon find out about the rest.

Gary tells me that Maj. Chandy and he were course mates, but the latter missed his selection board due to the accident. Pity the hotshot father couldn't fix that.

I head the PIT as the chief instructor of the course and

immediately under me is the senior instructor, Lt. Col Gary Randhawa, and instructors, Maj. Alex Anton and, now, Maj. George Chandy.

There are other chief instructors running different courses, but I pride myself in making real soldiers out of these prissy youngsters.

Four batches have passed out during my tenure – this is my last batch here. The good thing about the army is it doesn't let you stay in one place too long, lest the soldier gets too comfortable.

I have indeed become comfortable. It's a small station, like an island cut off from the mainland. A part of the army, yet not of it.

Brig. Sargam, the commandant of Jacob Hills, is an obnoxious man, but thankfully, he and I get along just fine.

My wife and children love the place. We live in a palatial, nineteenth-century bungalow built by the British. My office hours begin at eight and I am home for lunch.

The children are back from school and we eat in the lawn, soaking in the warmth of the sun while two men hover around, serving hot chapattis and keeping an eye out for bowls that need refilling.

The lawn is beautiful and the children have the freedom and space to play. I have built Bunny, my middle child, a doll house in the kitchen garden. She often likes to hide there when we play hide and seek. I always find her.

Bunny is my favourite. Parents always have a favourite,

no matter what they say about all children being equal. She turns six in a couple of months. It bothers me how fast they grow up. I don't want to give her away.

My oldest, Sunny, is eight and naughty as boys his age are. I am stern with him. I believe a boy never grows up to be a man without discipline.

Mini, my youngest, is three. She shies away from me and is not too prone to talking, always hanging on to her mother. When I wonder aloud why we bothered with a third child, my matric-pass wife is quick to remind me that I had always dreamt of a large family. They are right when they say, 'A man should be careful about what he dreams of.'

The next twenty minutes are the longest as Maj. Alex runs through his preachy speech on the role of an intelligence officer in an operational environment and how missing lectures is tantamount to sin.

Nobody ever taught him to keep it simple. Bloody bore! The boys have rightly named him Preacher Alex.

'Save the lecture for later,' I whisper to him.

Preacher Alex is not to be deterred. He stresses even harder on the importance of doing the right thing and making the army proud.

By the time the mike reaches me, I am mad as a bull.

'For the next eight months, you are entitled to no leave, no sleep and certainly no fucking rest! Someone is ill or dies in your family, send them your condolences – that's all that is going out of Jacob Hall. Do I make myself clear?'

The sleepy faces are attentive now. 'Do I make myself clear?' I repeat forcefully into the mike.

'Yes, sir, colonel!' comes the glass-shattering reply.

Back in my office, I ask for tea. My head is pounding and the day has not even begun. Akal Singh hands me a cup of tea without spilling some of it on the table, for a change.

He's my PA. Akal means intelligence, but he seems to possess none of it. The only reason I am stuck with this infuriating chap is that he is a distant country cousin of the brigadier's wife, who hails from Bareilly.

I curse Brig. Sargam often for making my life difficult, but in the army, there is this unspoken golden rule, 'Keep the boss happy and his wife happier.'

And I have every intention of making it to the next rank, so not only am I tolerant of his stupidity, I am kind and courteous, with the result that Akal Singh is all praise for me whenever he visits his fatso didi's house.

Not that Akal Singh's visits are encouraged much – it can't be too good for brigadier sahib to mingle with the ranks. Though the stories of him mingling with the maid servants are told in hushed tones.

The phone rings and it's the devil himself, my man Friday informs me.

'Howdy, colonel, how are the boys doing? I hear you gave them an earful.'

The ever-faithful Akal Singh must have used his akal and appraised the brigadier before transferring the call.

'Good morning, sir, just doing my job.'

'Good. I called you about the circular my office received from the Army Headquarters in Delhi, asking me to look into the conduct of an officer at Jacob Hall. The headquarters received an anonymous letter that some officer had been going around tongue-kissing young girls and stubbing out cigarettes on their tender flesh.'

'How young? Fifteen, sixteen?'

'No, we're talking little girls here, diapers and all. I will not stand this kind of nonsense in my area.'

The brigadier's concern for children is overwhelming, considering he has no children. The memsahib doesn't get pregnant, but the maidservants do. Three different girls who birthed daughters are said to resemble the brigadier.

This could be plain gossip or the gospel truth; one can never say – we are a nosy lot at Jacob Hills.

'Sir, Jacob Hills is like a swamp full of tadpoles! It's swarming with officers of all ranks round the year. It would be impossible to find someone without a name,' I tell the brigadier.

'Aren't you close to Col. Farhat, the Chief Instructor of the Skills at Arms course? Start with him ...'

'Colonel Farhat is an excellent chap, sir!'

'You bloody fellows don't listen! A little birdie says that his daughter had complained of some uncle who tried to kiss her in a party. Call him up and find out what happened.'

Why does all the shitty work fall my way? He could have just picked up the phone himself and asked Col. Farhat.

I have known him for many years, a religious chap and very useful, too. We often ask him to send us his instructors to give lessons in advanced weaponry to our YOs.

I postponed the call until lunch. Yet, the disturbing news kept playing on my mind. Who could have written a letter like that? A disgruntled wife or a jilted lover who had suffered at his hand? Such accusations are taken very seriously in the army – an officer could be court-martialed for such an offence.

I felt nervous. His daughter Junaira and Bunny were in the same class. What if someone were to write a letter about me? There is no way one can defend oneself against an unknown enemy writing accusatory letters.

I made the call.

Col. Farhat was delighted to hear from me and said, 'What can I do for you, Tehlan?'

I told him. A stretched silence followed, after which he dismissed the claim, saying it was nothing.

I persisted and he told me briefly that at a large gathering, his daughter had come running to him and said an uncle was trying to kiss her and when she had resisted, he burnt her with his cigarette.

'Why didn't you report it, sir?'

'My wife was hysterical, and later, when things became normal, she didn't want me to pursue it.'

'Why?'

'Our daughter will get married some day.'

'But she's only six!'

'This kind of a thing sticks. People have an amazing memory when it comes to gossiping about others' daughters. We don't want that kind of attention – the "You know what happened with Colonel Farhat's daughter" kind of thing.'

In a way, Col. Farhat is right. The army is no different from any other set-up. They are the same people, talking ill of others' wives and daughters.

I put the phone down and thought about my little girl.

Bunny is different, special. She never cries like other children.

She is my little princess, a princess who can play with the frog and not find him ugly.

The Body

George sent two Johnnies along, and they were busy opening cartons and emptying wooden boxes. He had unpacked the drums himself in the morning and set them up in the other room. George used to be a drummer in his college days. At times I get upset listening to stories about his glory days in the rock band that broke up after he joined the army.

He also wrote songs. Even now, once in a while, when the mood takes hold of him, he pens something overwhelming, like the lines he sang on my birthday:

What is this enchanting spell you cast?
This playful, teasing agony,
Sweet as the afternoon sleep,
Zingy as the lemon in my tea,
Musky as the steam from an old memory,
It must be the sun in your eyes,

That rises but never sets,
Not in my sky, it's here you shine the brightest, my
dove ...

I could not stop smiling for weeks after that.

Humming the song softly, I went to the kitchen. It was time to start cooking. For the past two weeks, we had eaten at other people's houses. The rich curries and spices the other wives used to make food palatable disgusted me. I had hiccupped through most of those evenings.

George found it amusing when I would begin to hiccup loudly, attracting a fair amount of unwanted attention, as soon as I put food in my mouth. I felt like disappearing when people rubbed my back, shoved glasses of water under my nose and looked at me with concern.

George joked, 'They are in awe of you. The delicate, blue-eyed Mrs Chandy and her enchanting hiccups – the life of the party!'

'If you are going to be mean to me, I won't invite anyone over.'

'Darling, please, just once. We'll have to. We have been pigging out at other people's homes since we came. Besides, once they sample your excellent culinary skills, I am convinced the desire to visit again will die down on its own.'

I did not speak to him for two hours after that – not until he finally apologized and made me a cup of my favourite black tea. He was right, my bland cooking could probably save us from hosting dinners that army protocol demands.

We liked our space, George and I, and his colleagues, though well-meaning, seemed like intruders. The invitations were always pouring in, and if you chose to RSVP, a phone call from the senior officer the next day would be enough to make you regret the quiet evening spent at home. So we often ended up attending these silly parties.

I met Mrs Sargam, George's boss's wife, last evening. She was an overbearing lady, who was quite pleased to know that I enjoyed singing. The next thing I knew, she was ordering me to prepare a song for Husbands' Night.

I enjoy singing, but I like to sing when I like to sing, and certainly not to a room full of inebriated men. George said it was up to me; I didn't have to sing if I didn't wish to. But Pam had a different take on it.

'You don't want to piss her off because if you do, she's likely to single you out every opportunity she gets, and there will be many.'

'I am an individual and it's my husband who is in the army, not me.'

'Don't be a fool, Eva. He may not go very far if you insist on maintaining your individuality.'

'You are saying my singing and dancing skills will determine my husband's future in the armed forces?'

'Silly as it may sound, the answer is yes.'

We both shared a hearty laugh and argued over which song should be sung for the event five weeks later.

I had come to terms with Pam's assertive personality and

had even started enjoying her company a little. Still, there were times I devised ways to be away from her. Luckily, she spent her evenings at the Tiller's Club playing squash with the officers. George can't play yet, so he watched after he was done swimming.

It was the only exercise he was allowed and the doctor said it would help strengthen his muscles. So my poor husband went swimming in this chilly weather. When I offered to accompany him he said, 'You need to warm me on my return from the pool.'

Oh, and it usually gets quite warm when he returns. George has a way of making even the most boring evening exciting. The dry wood in the backyard becomes a makeshift bonfire in the balcony. Conversation takes a backseat and we just sit there with our minds and bodies touching and sip brandy.

I like being kissed in the open. It's magical. The wetness of his mouth heightens as his hands crawl under my sweater to caress my stomach, gently moving down. The sting of the cold wind on my skin doesn't bother me. My body is burning from the brandy and the anticipation of what's to come, a teasing night of our bodies moving in a slow rhythm, his strong, warm thigh touching mine. Surprisingly, these quiet, unhurried moments have a strange intensity that even the wildest, kinkiest of coupling doesn't.

It does get a little eerie outdoors with jackals howling and strange noises coming from the forest. I hug him tight and sleep – there's no cuddle like an after-sex cuddle. I could spend my life on a mountain-top, just George and I. But he's more practical and wonders what we would eat after a particularly vigorous session of lovemaking if he didn't have a job. I despise him for a brief moment for spoiling my dream.

Finally, the house was set and there was food on the stove. I stepped out of the house to get some fresh air. I had spotted an old church on the hilltop past the Johnnies' quarters and the armament factory. I hoped to walk in that direction today.

The Johnnies' quarters were new but they don't look pretty, either because of a shoddy whitewash job or the rain. The women sat outside in circles, chatting, while the children played noisily in the big park ahead. I smiled as I passed them and hesitant smiles flashed back.

Soon after I started climbing, I caught a glimpse of the church. It was a strange structure that looked more like the Hindu temples one usually sees perched on mountain tops. I waded through the undergrowth and a garbage pile.

The garbage reminded me of a travelogue on India written by a foreigner. It said garbage heaps could be found everywhere in the country – from the remotest corner to the highest summit. The writer said garbage heaps were typical of the Indian people. I couldn't agree more as I stepped on used bags, footwear and broken plastic.

I pushed open the tall gate of the rundown church and hesitated momentarily, but the lure of the fine, stained-glass windows was far too great for me to abandon my exploration before it had begun. The glass was either broken or missing in places and the rays of the setting sun pierced the darkness poetically. Someone had begun painting a fresco of 'The Last Supper' above the altar. I stared at it for a while before moving on to the memorial plaques obscured by cobwebs.

I read the plaques as best as I could in the dark. Many familiar names from the British era as described in history books rang a bell. I hoped to drag George down here soon. It wouldn't be easy, architecture doesn't really inspire him, but maybe war history would. Yes, that's the angle that would work best with him.

I felt uneasy, the vibrations of the church were not positive, even though it was considered the abode of God. My mother often said that old places had their own energy. I felt it now; the cold and the dampness in the air gave me goosebumps.

In front of the altarpiece was a large black crucifix, about five feet tall and very wide. Spellbound, I moved closer.

An all-black centrepiece in a church is unheard of. At least, I had never come across something like this before. I walked past the pews and, as I was about to touch the crucifix, my hand froze mid-air as a fat drop of warm liquid fell on the back of my hand. I shuddered, thinking it could be anything from pigeon dropping to seepage.

I looked up to see if the roof was leaking; it wasn't. Unconsciously, I rubbed the place where the drop had fallen with my other hand. The sun was setting – it would be dark soon. I walked out hurriedly, leaving the rest of the inspection for another day.

It was a relief to be outside and catch the fading daylight. I became aware that someone was standing nearby, a man. He was wearing the games uniform: white shorts, white collared T-shirt, and white socks stretched up his calves. He was dark and good-looking, with hair slightly longer than most officers.

He even seemed familiar; the good-looking ones always do. Then I remembered that he was Maj. Alex, an instructor at the War College with George. We had met briefly at Brig. Sargam's dinner party a week ago.

He recognized me and wasn't happy to see me.

'What brings you here, Ma'am? There are all kinds of animals prowling around the area. You see that den there? People say a leopard lives there.'

It did look like a place a leopard would like to savour his kill, but the tone of Maj. Alex's voice sounded more angry than concerned.

But I was not to be deterred.

'I was fascinated by the church and just came by to take a look. Have you seen the black crucifix? It's unusual, even macabre, don't you think?'

'The church was abandoned in 1867, soon after it was

built at the insistence of Sir Jacob Dunhill. He was fascinated by the Indian Goddess Kali and the old temples built in caves. They say he was a little crazy and made the local populace build the church so that it resembled a temple. People thought it was bad to mess around with religion.'

'What about the crucifix?'

'The crucifix, they say, is made of solid cast brass, but it turned black after the body of a young girl was found on the church's premises, half-eaten by jackals. People stopped going to the church after the maintenance staff found mangled bodies of birds and small animals at the same place where they had found the body of the girl. It spooked them.'

'The animals attacked the girl?'

'No, the locals say that she was murdered and left to die. She wasn't from these parts, so no one came to claim the body.'

'I wonder what could have happened.' From where I stood, I could see the black crucifix.

'Some British officer seduced the young maid, murdered her and dumped the body here, I suppose.'

'What about the crucifix turning black?'

'Some kind of metallurgical reaction, maybe. You don't believe in ghosts, do you?'

'Did they find the man who killed the girl?' I couldn't help myself, although I could tell that he was getting impatient with all my questions.

'No, they didn't. It was as easy to take a life a century ago as it is now.'

'Life can't be stubbed out at the whim of men. All life is His to give – or take.'

His face grew sombre.

It was getting late and I extended my hand to say goodbye. He shook it lightly and then pulled it towards him, alarming me a little.

'Are you hurt?'

'No.' I tried to pull my hand out of his grasp.

'There's blood on your hand.' He turned my hand a little so I could see better. There was a drop of semi-dried blood on it.

'Oh, it fell from the roof.'

He stared at me.

'I was near the altarpiece when it fell. Maybe there is an injured bird or animal on the roof. Should we go and check?'

He turned abruptly and I followed him into the church and up the stairs to the roof. It was dark, the pigeons kept flying at us. God, what was I doing here – alone, with a man I barely knew? I wanted to leave, but worried about what Maj. Alex think.

We reached the top, panting. The sun had set and I couldn't see much. I kept looking back at the den, not wanting to be surprised by a hungry leopard.

There was a strange hum in the air. 'Shhh, did you hear

that?' I asked my companion. The sound was coming from the area that was directly above the crucifix. We inched closer.

She lay there, bleeding. Her shallow breathing bouncing off the walls of the church.

I simply froze, but Alex knelt by her side and checked her pulse. I stood at a distance, baffled. It had been *her* blood on my hand. The blood oozed from her stomach like a hot spring. Her cotton sari stuck to her frail body. Her hair was tied in a loose bun, and there were remnants of red vermillion on her scalp.

I tried to see her face, but Alex had already scooped the girl up in his arms. Her eyes were open, but whatever it was she was seeing, it wasn't us.

'Ma'am, you'll have to run down to the Johnnies' quarters and get help. Get a vehicle. I will follow you,' Alex said to me.

'I will.' Yet, I stood there, looking at her, wondering what would have happened if the leopard had found her before we did.

I heard Alex shout, 'I could go, but then you'll have to stay with her.'

'No! I'll get help.'

I started to run. My feet felt heavy as I ran down the slope, fast as I could. I stopped at the bottom. There were so many people walking by, for a moment I stood there wondering what to say. I felt silly screaming for help, but the image of the girl's body covered in blood pushed me to scream.

'Help me, please!' A small crowd gathered around me.

'Someone's badly injured at the church. I need a vehicle, any vehicle, please!'

A truck driver offered to come with me. A senior sergeant rushed to make a phone call. I told him to also inform George at the Tiller's Club to meet me at the Military Hospital.

A few Johnnies jumped into the back while I sat in front with the driver. It was pitch-dark by now and there weren't any street lights on the slope. Midway, we saw Alex walking down the slope carrying the girl, his white shirt soaked with her blood. He gently placed her in the back and I finally saw her face.

I was shocked to see the girl's body had the face of a mature woman. It was pinched; pain seemed to be an old friend of hers. All I could tell was that she had a stomach wound. It was tough to tell more through her sari, which had once been pastel blue but was now dyed red.

As soon as we reached the hospital she was wheeled in to the operating theatre. I stayed back and soon Maj. Alex disappeared. I stood in the foyer, lost.

Half an hour later, there was still no sign of anyone. I sat facing the corridor, waiting for someone to bring news of what was going on behind closed doors. A nurse with a stern face walked past without looking at me.

'Excuse me, is she going to be all right?'

The nurse walked up to where I stood and asked me in earnest, 'Are you with the lady?'

She was curvy, with dimpled cheeks and a competent air.

'Can you tell me how she got burnt?'

'Burnt? I thought she was wounded ...'

'How are you related to her?'

'I am not. We found her at the abandoned church and brought her here.'

'Goodness me, what were you doing at the old church? That's no tourist spot. Are you with the man who admitted her?'

'Yes. No. He's my husband's colleague.'

My hasty defence must have appeared strange to her. Certainly no lady of repute would go to an abandoned place with her husband's colleague. She gave me a knowing smile and left.

I walked through another corridor in search of Maj. Alex and found him sitting on a bench, holding his head in his hands. His body rocked slightly and I heard him mumble something that sounded like the Hail Mary.

How many devout Catholic men would pray for an unknown woman? I left him to his prayers and came back to the lobby.

It was seven in the evening, and still no sign of George. I suspected the sergeant had failed to inform him. I looked around the reception desk for a phone; there was no one behind it. An old song was playing on the radio from a room a little further. I peeped in and found the same nurse

I had met earlier, drinking a cup of tea and massaging her forehead.

'Is there a phone I could use?'

She pointed to a phone, an olive green instrument the size of a bread loaf that connected the hospital to the rest of the cantonment – it's like the one we have at home. I mumbled a thank you and called home, but there was no response.

I dialled the operator's number and asked him to connect me to the Tiller's Club, but they said George had left an hour ago.

Where was George? He was usually home by seven. God, I hoped he wasn't out looking for me; any kind of stress was bad for him.

I sat on the chair, feeling and looking miserable. The next thing I knew, the stiff-lipped nurse offered me a cup of watery coffee. I took a big sip and thanked her, yet again.

'Wilhelmina,' she introduced herself.

'That's a lovely name. I am Eva Chandy. My husband recently got posted as an instructor at the training school.'

'Which course?'

'The PIT.'

'Oh. The young buggers from the PIT course are always coming down here with a sprain or fever to get excused from the day's lecture so they can ride to Shimla to mate, uh ... meet with their girlfriends.'

I smiled.

'One cheeky bugger asked me out once too! You know how they have a thing for older women.'

'You are not old.'

'I don't look it but trust me, sweetie, I've been around.'

I liked how she called me 'sweetie' within minutes of our brief acquaintance.

'Anyway, I had a day off, so I said why not. Well, he rode like the devil himself and nearly broke my neck, not to mention the sudden breaks that had me clinging to him for dear life. I vowed never to go out again with these twenty-somethings. They can't wait to have your boobs rubbing their back.'

Boy, that was crude, but it made me smile.

'I should tell you something of what these YOs are up to, thinking they are God's greatest gift to women, around to squeeze as much juice as they can out of life.'

I laughed at Wilhelmina's choice of words. She was chatty once she opened up, and that's how I got to know that there was a vacancy for an English teacher in the army school. The principal, Mrs Farhat, was a nice lady and in desperate need for someone to manage the first grade.

I made a mental note to visit the school soon. I asked Wilhelmina about the girl's condition.

'The wound has led to perforation of the abdominal aorta and there is considerable intra-abdominal haemorrhage. They are stitching her up now, but the word is she won't make it through the night.'

'You said in the foyer that she's got burns?'

'Oh, they are old, near the chest and the vaginal area. Years of abuse. Probably the same bastard who left her there to die.'

Burn marks near the vaginal area? Wilhelmina said it casually, as if such cases were routine for her.

The buzzer in the room rang. She gulped her coffee and rushed out.

The waiting game began all over again for me. George came in close to nine, his face flushed with anger. He didn't say a word to me; instead he spoke to Maj. Alex, who miraculously appeared by my side not five minutes before George arrived. It must have seemed as if we had been chatting away, while George spent the last hour searching every nook and cranny of Jacob Hills for his wife.

We left for home in the official jeep. He hadn't been on his Bullet since the accident, which restricted our movements greatly.

He disliked calling the driver to take him around during his off-duty hours. He was cut from a different cloth – his peers had no qualms misusing government machinery.

George unlocked the wooden door, pushed the mesh door open and stood in the living room, facing me.

'I can walk around. I am not crippled that I can't fulfil your whim to wander around town.'

'George, I went there on an impulse and realized my mistake the moment I got there. I am sorry; I did try to send a message across.'

'I have been waiting, worrying, wondering if something had happened to you. I finally asked for the jeep. The duty officer wanted to know why, but I could hardly tell him that I was looking for my wife!'

'I tried to call you, you weren't answering the phone.'

'Must have been in the bathroom or something. How the hell did you bump into Alex?'

'I met him at the church and I am glad I did, otherwise we never would have found the woman.'

'He's a decorated soldier, but a loony character – that's what I've heard. Stay away from him, Eva. For all you know, it could have been Alex who stabbed the woman and left her there. And then he saw you and rushed to assist another damsel in distress.'

'Oh, George, you have this really nasty habit of being suspicious of everyone.'

He marched to the bedroom and shut the door.

George wasn't himself. Something was bothering him, something that had nothing to do with me.

I stared at the blue flame from the gas stove wearily. The evening's events were blurry, but the mind has an innate ability to filter the important bits and pieces from the mundane.

I had called home from the hospital every fifteen minutes since the clock struck seven. Surely, he couldn't have been in the bathroom all that while? George had lied about waiting for me at home.

George

Piranha in the Pond

The blackboard was blank, I stared at it a moment longer. When I was certain that the YO running late for the morning lecture had jumped into the classroom through the big window and had taken his seat, I turned to address my students. I don't believe in unnecessary showdowns. He was most welcome to dig his own grave; I'd simply give him an F.

These young men were supposed to have come to class prepared with a 'battle presentation'. Obviously I chose the smug bastard who had just jumped in through the window to present a war story first.

Capt. Rana swaggered to the pulpit, scratched his nose, cleared his throat and ill-prepared as he was, chose to speak about Second Lieutenant Arun Khetarpal.

Every patriot knew about this hero of the 1971 Indo-Pak War, whose bravery inspired many a misguided youth to serve his country, including me. I knew his story by heart.

Rana spoke haltingly, sometimes at a total loss for words. His Rambo-like jaw shook indecisively, but he got the show going. A confident chap; I had to grant him that much.

'During the 1971 war, the 17 Poona Horse of the Indian Army was intent on establishing a bridgehead across the River Basantar. The area was extensively mined, which prevented the regiment from deploying its tanks. The engineers clearing the mines were halfway through their tasks when Indian troops at the bridgehead reported alarming activity of the enemy armour. The commander of Squadron B radioed for urgent reinforcement.

'At 0800 hours, on December 16th, the Pakistani armour and infantry unit launched a counterattack on 17 Poona Horse stationed at Jarpal in the Shakargarh sector. The commander of Squadron A, Lieutenant Khetarpal, was stationed nearby and answered the radio call. He marched forward with his detachment of two tanks and troops. Khetarpal rushed to meet the Pakistani armour as the situation in the Squadron B sector grew tense.

'Khetarpal and his troops crossed the Basantar and came under fire from enemy RCL (recoilless) gun nests that were holding out. Lieutenant Khetarpal responded by attacking the enemy strong points head on. His tanks even captured a few of the enemy infantry and weapons crew at pistol point, but during the attack, the commander of the second tank took a hit. Khetarpal wasn't disheartened. He relentlessly pursued the enemy till he broke through the sector, only to find the enemy tanks pulling back.

'Khetarpal didn't allow them a peaceful retreat. He chased them and gunned down an enemy tank. The enemy retreated, but only for a while, and regrouped to attack Lieutenant Khetarpal's sector. A fierce tank combat ensued in which ten enemy tanks were hit, of which Khetarpal destroyed four.

'He was hit by enemy fire and severely wounded, but he did not abandon his tank. He destroyed another tank that was barely hundred metres away. At that point, his tank was hit a second time and he was mortally injured. All was not lost that day. His bravery strengthened the position of the Indian Army in the Shakargarh sector and not one Pakistani tank could make it through. Lieutenant Khetarpal was awarded the highest wartime gallantry award, the Param Vir Chakra, posthumously.'

I was mildly surprised to find that the audience was not merely attentive, but riveted.

'Good show, Rana. I didn't expect you to get the details right.'

Emboldened by his success, Capt. Rana said, 'Sir, I am yet to share the most interesting part.'

'Well, don't keep us waiting, Captain.'

'It is reported that Khetarpal's final words to a superior officer ordering him to abandon his tank when hit, were, "No, sir, I will not abandon my tank. My gun is still working and I will get these bastards."'

A huge applause followed to honour the valour of a man who had been dead fifteen years. This kind of courage in the face of death was something that could not be taught in a classroom.

We can teach them to shoot, to kill. We can produce good soldiers, but we can't make heroes out of them. Khetarpal had joined the army, just as his father had. The second and third generation soldiers knew the price their fathers and forefathers had paid for our independence.

I saw the spirit of patriotism fleetingly brush their youthful faces. I was impressed but only for a while, sure that inside an hour it would be pushed to the back of their minds. Or maybe it was just me; I had become jaded with time.

I was commissioned only after the Indo-Pak war of 1971 – there were heavy casualties on both sides. It is said that during the thirteen-day war, the Pakistani soldiers raped thirty thousand women in Bangladesh, all Hindus.

I remember my father had returned home a distraught man, having attended too many funerals. Many homes lost their sons, brothers and husbands – the anti-Pakistan sentiment ran high.

I was all of nineteen, just out of college, and passionate about serving the country. A bunch of us sat for the exam and cleared it too.

I had been in service for fourteen years and I had not seen any war, neither was I likely to; the days of good old battles were over. It was the beginning of a coward's war, the rise of the new-age terrorist, who attacked innocent civilians and disappeared.

At thirty-three, my aspirations were very different from what they had been a decade ago. I was now quite content with being a musician.

The decibel in the classroom was rising, so I asked them to maintain order, else show themselves out.

If they wished to attend my lecture on strategy and war games, *they* must make the effort, not me. I didn't believe in screaming my throat hoarse to ensure discipline, nor was I bothered with maintaining the PIT's spotless record – I'd rather fail some of these worthless buggers. More often than not, they would be the ones who would end up as generals.

Kissing ass was not an art openly encouraged in the army, but one develops a taste for it sooner rather than later. Gary was a classic example. He would never call on a senior officer at their house without 'a little token', such as handcrafted mojris from Ludhiana for the colonel's wife, famous laddoos from Lovely Sweet House in Jalandhar, or a semi-nude painting of a couple that could grace the colonel's living room.

I had nothing against these seemingly innocent gestures, but they raised the bar for the other officers. Not everyone liked to carry gifts when returning from their home towns, nor did all officers like the thought of their wives gushing over their seniors.

So while the Garys of the world made a place for themselves in the army, men like me were labelled as 'dry' officers and in time got superseded.

'Egos have to be fed and pampered if one wishes to rise in life,' my old man had once said to me. He didn't like the idea of a general's son being sent home as a major. Well, I am not cut out for it, the 'yes, sir, yes, sir, I'll kiss your ass, sir!'

As I stood by the window, I was tempted to go out – the noise was driving me up the wall.

'Be quiet or a twenty-mile run in the sun will fix your fucking libidos!'

They lowered their pitch, but I could still hear snatches of conversation. My curiosity was piqued. They were talking about Alex.

'Father Alex doesn't drink or smoke and the joke is he would simply leak at the thought of touching a woman, and you are saying he was with two of them?' I heard Rana ask another YO, a Capt. Joshi.

'He was fooling around with this Anglo girl on the roof of that rundown church and found this other woman there, bleeding. They are saying his shirt was covered in blood by the time he got her to the hospital.'

'What about the Anglo girl?'

'That one is something! I had gone to see Panda at the hospital this morning. He told me she was all hot and sexy, chewing on her fine nails and waiting for Father Alex in the hospital lobby.'

'Could be some stuffy brigadier's daughter visiting during school break, and boring Alex must have taken her sightseeing to the old church.'

'Find her, Rana, and you can show her the delights that Jacob Hills has to offer.'

'Buddy, I'll bet you a hundred she'll have the time of her life because I won't be delivering anything lame, sermons or otherwise,' was Rana's cocky reply.

I wanted to get up and break his long nose and Rambo jaw, but he didn't know it was my wife he was talking about. There seemed no point in fuelling the rumour mills; their filthy minds had already turned an innocuous incident into a romp.

Men in their twenties can't see past a woman's body. It's not just their oversized pricks; it's their inflated egos. So they talk dirty and boast about their mostly imaginary conquests to impress each other.

It took all of my self-control not to react, but I made a mental note to warn Eva to stay away from Alex, yet again.

It was not going to be easy. Alex had found a little place in Eva's large heart by playing the Good Samaritan. I love my wife, but she can be quite naive.

I needed to smoke. It had been six months since I had lit a cigarette. Hell, I really needed one now!

I came out to smoke and stood under a grand oak, the cigarette puff spread like rhapsody to my head.

The peace and quiet lasted exactly five minutes and then Gary took the cigarette from my hand and took a drag.

'Beautiful building, isn't it?'

We both looked admiringly at the stone building of the War College that stretched into the east wing, which housed the Mess and the barracks and the west wing, where the lectures took place. The central building had the commandant's office and the administrative wing; the place was quiet like a mausoleum.

The training ground was right in front of the office block twice the size of a football field. A few officers in combat gear climbed the monkey rope in the glaring sun. The firing range was at a distance on a hillock and a target practice session was on.

To one side was the common prayer area, where a Hanuman temple, a gurudwara and a pir-fakir's mazar were looked after by the soldiers. One of the most incredible things about the army is that it is truly secular. Men from different faiths work side by side like brothers. I was a little sentimental about the soldiers; they were simple men from small villages who sometimes never went back home. I remembered the men I had lost. 'Mizo National Army blew up a military truck, killing ten', that's all the newspapers had reported, ten nameless men who faded into oblivion. I inhaled deeply and let out the smoke.

Gary said, 'There is a working lunch at one. Did you get that circular?'

'Oh, no, I was looking forward to an afternoon nap.'

'Since when did you start napping in the afternoon? Oh,

I see! Only your leg is injured, the rest of you is working fine.' He winked at me.

'Gary, you don't think beyond the stomach and the two inches below it.'

'Sorry, partner, that's all I live for, the sins of the flesh. An afternoon quickie hurts no one.'

He left and I pulled out another stick and thought about Gary and Pam, rather Gurinder Singh and Parminder Kaur.

Back in the seventies, Gary would joke that the army is the only profession where smoking and drinking is encouraged and even commands a certain respect in society.

He would also be heard saying that all that an officer needed – food, uniform, boots and a buddy – was issued by the army, and if a wife had been really necessary, the army would have made her also an issue item.

And so it is that Gary drank, smoked and played the field for a long time before marrying into a wealthy family. He had liberal ideas and he did not hesitate to implement them. It was no surprise that he was far ahead of all his course mates.

He had a pretty wife, a four-year-old son and a great career ahead. I had envied him for a long time, but last evening put paid to all the envy. The scene from Gary's living room flashed in my mind.

'I love you.' Pam batted her eyelids coyly.

'Are you out of your mind? I have a wife.'

'Fair enough, Georgy.'

'What do you mean fair enough, Pam?'

'I just want to be with you.'

'We are both married, and not to each other, or have you forgotten?'

'Aw, you take your vows too seriously, Georgy.'

'Pam, stop flirting with me, I am not good at this. Where is the coffee and where is Gary?'

I pretended to be bored, but she saw through me like one who knows when a child is telling a lie.

'He won't be back for another hour, so I'll have to do all the entertaining.'

'Aren't you afraid that I might tell Gary?'

'No, why, should I be?'

She smiled and went in to the kitchen, while I sweated. There was chemistry here, and danger too.

I had heard stories of her fooling around with the YOs. But men are men and they liked to misread innocent gestures. Her gestures were pretty clear last evening. That was definitely a proposition and an indecent one at that.

I couldn't wait to finish my coffee and leave. What happened to the demure and timid Pam of six years ago? In those days, she wore salwar suits with tiny, flowery prints, covered her head with a dupatta and every other sentence ended with 'haan ji'.

The behenji from Punjab had come a long way. Was Gary behind this transformation? No, I don't think so. He's an ambitious man, but he wouldn't use Pam to further his career. That wasn't Gary's style. And in their relationship, Pam wore the pants. Her new avatar owed more to the British legacy of the club and its party culture.

Before she married Gary, Pam would have never seen huge gatherings where one interacted with the opposite sex freely, drank, danced and dressed to flaunt one's body.

The world over, the hippie movement has been on a roll since the sixties. There is progressive thinking – premarital sex – but our society, even in the eighties, is stuck in a rut. The Indian middle class is far too rigid to allow men and women to come together openly. Marriage is the legal, societal sanction that a couple requires to give in to their biological urges.

A result of all these social and religious taboos against sex before marriage is that both men and women stumble through their first night together.

I recall this hilarious story of a honeymoon where the groom spent night after night consoling his grief-stricken bride that it was not a sin to part her legs for her husband.

Once the deed is done, the man is relieved that he can now safely lay claims to his manhood and be a part of the men's club, while a woman is left baffled by the whole act.

It is supposed to be an act of pleasure, the coming together of two souls and all she experiences is pain and a sense of ridicule and alienation.

Then there are the 'fast' women who give in to their sexual urges sans the mangalsutra and suffer the shame of being called whores.

Of course, the men too face sexual repression; a boy cannot even deliver a love letter to a girl or hold her hand without risking the ire of her folks, brothers and the entire neighbourhood. And so he's left to play with himself till he reaches a ripe age and his parents marry him off, fearing for his sanity.

There are many perversions in our society – the arranged marriage not the least of them. Two people are joined for life, whether they like it or not. The marriage has to be saved, adjustments have to be made. For the majority, this arrangement of sex for financial security works very well and they go on to have several children. Brilliant, isn't it? Like an island in this stiff social structure is the army, with its 'free' and elite lifestyle, with its exclusive clubs, swimming pools, and parties where men and women mingle freely. The kind of dream an ordinary Indian man or woman only sees in the movies.

I know for a fact that before joining the academy, quite a few of the men have neither held a fork and a knife, nor had the slightest idea what to do with a dinner napkin. The army trains and polishes them, but what it can't change is their rustic roots. There is a popular joke in the army, 'Angrez chale gaye, par inhe chhod gaye,' the British may have gone but they left these idiots behind. The 'idiots' are the overeager officers and their wives who, in a bid to appear modern, ape the lifestyle of the more sophisticated ones.

Men adapt far more easily than the women. The army motto is befitting, 'Do you have it in you?' The men certainly have it in them, and they are quick to mould themselves into its drinking-smoking-womanizing culture.

However, the behenjis are up against the more educated, city-bred wives and don't have it easy. The low-cut maxis and blouses held together by thin strings are a shortcut to appear smart and educated. Their lack of eloquence is more than made up for by their revealing clothes.

And for the officers, any woman is fair game. Of course, it's all proper and highly civilized, but underneath all that chivalry lurks the animal instinct. Outside the norms of the regressive society, this setting becomes a trawling ground for men and women satiating their basest desires.

The Key Club was one such gathering. The officers got together to taste not just whisky, but each other's wives. The organization was in no way responsible for this; like in every profession, one fish was enough to spoil the pond. Jacob Hills was one such pond, and Pam, a piranha in it.

Captain Rana

The Fart Bomb

'I am done! This stupid operation plan can wait till the night. There's lamb for lunch, people!'

The class is more than happy to drift towards the east wing.

I walk down the stairs as the officers push past in a hurry to get to the Mess. It's madness during lunchtime and the sooner you get to the table, the brighter your chances of finding a little flesh on the bone. Otherwise, it's just a bowl of leftovers. Because of our rigorous schedule, by noon, it's difficult to contain the hunger pangs. So work can bloody wait.

But it's not work that's on my mind. I'm desperate to find a place where I can take Heena and not be bothered by the curious locals. The moment the nosey bastards see a girl as pretty as Heena walking with a man, not only are they protective but threatening, a situation from which even my army training can't save me.

We can't even stroll on Mall Road without one of her many bhai-jans spotting us. So we walk around as strangers, visiting the cathedral or riding to Kufri. I want to touch her, kiss her.

She must feel the same. I can tell by the way she holds me tightly when we are on the Bullet. But all this holding only fuels the fire. I am tired of these games, I want to feel her.

Let's see, tomorrow is Saturday. She can bunk the morning practical. If the Circuit House booking comes through, we can spend the weekend there. It's going to be a little tricky – we'll have to pretend to be husband and wife, but that's all right. What is life without a little risk?

I think I must be in love to go to such great lengths to book a place and risk my career. But her long hair and those trusting eyes haunt my dreams. I want to be inside her.

Another big hurdle is the morning lecture – I'll have to skip it and hope no one raises a fuss. Tomorrow's schedule will be up on the board only this evening. I hope it's not Randhawa's or Preacher Alex's class. Both will have my ass for missing their lecture. The new instructor Chandy is my man. He doesn't seem the hell-raising kind.

With all this on my mind, I steer clear of my course mates. Even if one of them gets a whiff of what I am planning, the news will spread like wildfire. No, the story of my escapade can wait. I'll tell them later. Of course, it's a big thing out here, to sleep with a woman.

Most of these losers have never seen a woman naked

except in the English movies or blue films at the academy. I have had my share of experiences, but not as many as I would like. Oh, well, I am just twenty-three; the world is my mating ground!

The dining area is a huge hall with long tables that shine spotlessly. The tables are allocated course- and seniority-wise, so there is no confusion about who will sit where. The waiters are laying food on the table, and the sound of tinkling forks and spoons and conversation is heavy on the ears. My plans to seduce Heena are put on hold.

I ask someone to pass me lamb, watery but tasty, even if it is more bones than flesh.

Capt. Panda walks in and sits next to me, the swelling on his forehead the size of a tennis ball.

'Panda, they discharged you! But am sorry to say, pal, you don't look any better.'

Panda is a dumb fellow. He walked into the door after drinking too much a few nights ago. His head was bleeding so profusely we had to rush him to the hospital in the middle of the night. It turned out to be a superficial cut, but Panda insisted that he be kept under observation. Moron.

Joshi asks Panda, 'Has the woman regained consciousness or has the Alex effect not yet worn off?'

There is laughter. The story of Preacher Alex making out with two women and nearly killing one during the course of things was doing the rounds, courtesy Panda.

The bell rings and chairs are pushed back hurriedly for a quick fag before class begins. I am still hungry and take a last serving of rice before screaming at the waiter to get me some lamb from the kitchen. The waiter returns with a bowl full of juicy lamb. Panda looks at me with puppy eyes and I grudgingly leave some pieces of lamb for him.

We eat in silence. The bell rings again, no time for a fag. I get up and so does Panda.

I walk fast. This was one class I didn't want to miss.

'Slow down, Rana, what's the rush?'

'We'll be late for Fart Bomb's class.'

'That's what you guys call him?'

'No, it's what he calls himself. Now, hurry up.'

Panda is confused; he wasn't there for the first lecture yesterday. We reach the classroom and grab the last seats. Pansy Panda sits next to me. The senior instructor from the Skills at Arms course walks in with a briefcase in his hand.

He's stout and looks at us from over his thick glasses before running his fingers over a bushy moustache and saying a loud, 'Good afternoon class, I am Colonel Padha.'

There is muffled laughter from the back and someone makes a fart noise, but Col. Padha is least affected. He opens his briefcase, takes out a few notes and begins the lecture.

The students in front furiously jot down every word, while we, the backbenchers, talk in hushed tones.

'He's so stiff-lipped,' says Pansy Panda.

'I would be too, if I had a name like that,' I reply.

I make a few fart sounds and the next thing I know, Fart Bomb is asking me to leave the class.

'Sir, but that wasn't me.'

'Captain, what do you think you are being punished for?'

'Sorry, sir.'

'Do you have an upset stomach?'

A sheepish grin is all I can manage.

'I'll take it as a yes. Take your ass down to the toilet and let the class breathe easy. Isn't there a foul smell in the air?'

He looks at my companion pointedly. A nervous Panda immediately replies, 'Yes, sir!'

So I have no choice but to walk out of class, grinning faces looking at me as I pass them. Col. Padha hasn't had his last word so he calls out, 'I could have a word with Chief Instructor Tehlan if the problem with your stomach persists. Can't have you farting in my face for the rest of the course.'

The Dead and the Dying

I sat on a bench outside the principal's office and waited for her to call me in. My lines were well rehearsed and I was all set to impress her with my degree in English literature, confident that she would take one look at my qualifications and offer me the job.

I was called in. The office was neat. A large wooden desk separated her from me. Mrs Farhat, clad in a green salwaar kameez, offered me a seat.

We made polite conversation while she went through my certificates.

I had expected her to look thrilled, but she wasn't.

'It's very impressive, Mrs Chandy, but I am afraid the vacancy is to teach the first and second grade and I am not sure how interested you are in wiping runny noses and taking children to the toilet, other than teaching them English.'

'Madam, that wouldn't be a problem.'

'Let me warn you, these children aren't very well mannered and they don't understand a word of English because their parents don't speak any at home. And of the forty students in the class, thirty-five are children of the jawans. It's a multilingual nightmare.'

'I could try.'

'Think again. The previous teacher left without notice. She found the experience harrowing and, frankly speaking, it doesn't look like your cup of tea.'

'You will not be disappointed, Madam.'

She studied my face, taking in my pale skin, blue eyes and the long wavy hair. I knew what she was thinking: here comes an Englishwoman wanting to teach the less privileged, the underdogs.

It's hard to explain to judgemental people like her how much I love being around children. It doesn't matter whose children they are. Everybody around Jacob Hills suffered from a rank-complex – the officers' children, the jawans' children. What is the big deal? Children are children, aren't they?

She told me to join from Monday, politely accepting my exuberant gratitude.

I climbed into the jeep and asked the driver how far the hospital was. He pointed to a white building down the hill. It was close by, so I decided to walk down.

'I'll walk. You can go back, thank you.' But the driver still insisted.

Memsahibs didn't ordinarily walk in the sun – especially not when their husbands were entitled to a vehicle. It was a big thing, if your husband's appointment came with a telephone and a vehicle. A status symbol most wives liked to flaunt.

I dismissed him.

During the day, the hospital was abuzz with activity. There was a long line of patients outside the OPD and their relatives occupied chairs in the lobby. The reception was manned by a male nursing assistant. He told me that my patient was on the critical list in the ICU.

I went in search of Wilhelmina. She was happy to see me and I gave her the good news about my job. She was in a hurry, though, so I quickly asked her how the lady was doing.

'The doctors have stitched her up, but she's lost too much blood and there is a fifty-fifty chance. A pity her family isn't here. We have notified the Military Police in Shimla. They checked with the local police, but no missing person's report has been filed.'

'How is it that she's not being missed? Could she be from the village?'

'No idea, but she's regained consciousness and should be able to give us something soon.'

'Oh, Wilhelmina, can I see her?'

'Sweety, no one is really allowed to see her till the police come and take her statement. It's a police case, you know, and if she dies, it's murder then.'

I had to really plead with Wilhelmina to let me into the ICU. She was quite obstinate, but relented when I said, 'Imagine, no one to say a kind word to you when you are taking your last breath.'

She asked me to remove my shoes, spoke to the nurse outside the ICU, opened the door for me and asked me to be out in ten minutes.

'The last bed on the right.'

I walked past patients, some comatose, others crying out in pain. The occupant of the last bed stared unseeingly outside the window. The view of the hills was obscured by another building, but she seemed to be looking beyond it.

Her head was tilted to the side and her body looked frail in the white sheets of the big hospital bed. I stood beside her bed.

Eventually, I cleared my throat to say, 'Don't worry, you'll be all right soon.'

It was a funny thing to say to someone who was not likely to make it and maybe that was why my words lacked conviction. She was barely a few years older than I.

I tried again. 'Is there anything I can do? Call someone, your parents, husband, children ...' I trail off.

'I have no children,' she said softly.

'I was at the church when you ... We carried you here.'

A shadow of fear flickered in her eyes when I mentioned the church.

'What happened to you at the church?' I probed, gently.

She was about to say something, but changed her mind and instead lifted her gown up to her waist slowly, painfully, to show what she couldn't describe.

The zigzag stitches from the operation were raw and red. I closed my eyes and opened them again. Other than the fresh wound, there were ghastly burn marks on her body. Like pockmarks, they travelled all the way down from her navel. They were ugly – black and blue, old and new.

I could not suppress the nausea rising inside and for a moment cursed myself for walking in here. The feeling passed, and anger swelled in my body and mind.

'Who did this to you?'

She quickly pulled her gown down and turned away from me.

'This man deserves to be punished! Who is he?'

I walked to the other side of the bed and found tears rolling down her cheeks like silent cries of pain. The pain she had bottled deep inside, the pain of being abandoned, of being unloved. She reminded me of a stray dog with scabies, lying on the roadside, pink skin exposed and bleeding in places; ignored by pedestrians, she snoozes in the sun, waiting to die.

I looked at her crooked fingers that may have been broken at some point in time. Where the IV entered her vein, the skin had turned blue. How much could a person endure?

I didn't know much about pain, I had a very loving

childhood. I knew even less about the other kind of pain; my relationships had brought me immense happiness, from my parents, siblings and George.

The concept of pain was new to me. The most I had experienced was a restless night if George and I had an argument – he was always the first to apologize. I imagined myself in her place, in her shoes, in her scars ... It was a blood-curdling thought.

I was blessed to have it all: a supportive family and a loving husband, who would miss me and grieve for me if anything were to happen to me. Sitting there, holding her hand, these thoughts clouded my mind.

She was delirious and kept drifting in and out of sleep, so I couldn't believe my ears when, in a quivering voice, she began to hum.

'Khanchar bhitor ochin pakhi kaymne ashe jay ...'

I was mesmerized by her voice. I had grown up in Calcutta and understood the sweet music of Bengal. But she was not from Bengal, the accent wasn't right and the beautiful Bong eyes were missing.

She sang the same line over and over, like a child who knows only the first line of a favourite nursery rhyme.

Tears pricked my eyes as she fell silent at last. I didn't have the heart to leave her. Strange, how different God has made men and women. I have never known a woman to harm anyone so deeply, but there are countless stories of atrocities committed by men against women. I desperately wanted to know what had gone wrong in her life, why she was here and dying all alone.

She died in her sleep. Wilhelmina found me like that, holding her hand. I looked at the woman's face, filled with fear even in death. Would there be peace for her in another world? All her earthly desires were yet to be fulfilled; I had seen the longing in her eyes when I asked about children.

Could a soul like that find peace, even in the house of God? That night, I had my first brush with pain. I clung to George and told him how much I loved him and that I was grateful to him for returning my love.

We take each other's love for granted, expecting the give and take of marriage to keep the love alive. George is right. Love isn't an agreement on paper. It's not even a promise and certainly not a responsibility. It is the song that the heart hums not knowing how or why. I kissed George and sang her song in his ears.

'What does it mean?' George asked, his head propped up on his elbow.

'It's a song by the famous Bengali poet Lalon, it means "the unknown bird in the cage, how does it fly in and out?"'

'Khanchar bhitor ochin pakhi kaymne ashe jay ...'

George had left by the time I woke up the next morning. I found a boiled egg on a plate and bread in the toaster. My husband is a self-sufficient man in no particular need of my wifely duties. George would function very well without me, I think.

I ate the toast and egg and walked about the house, fixing things. When the clock struck eleven, I went to take a quick shower; the batman would be here anytime. We liked our privacy, so unlike other families, the batman didn't stay in the servant's quarter. He came in every day for a couple of hours to run errands like buying vegetables and groceries from the store, giving clothes for ironing and other routine chores.

The day just went by. I looked through my closet for something suitable to wear for my first day at school. George was amused by my bordering-on-silly excitement, but I didn't expect him to understand the joy of reporting to your first job. He had been working since he left college, while I was being groomed to be a lady at home. Only, being a lady can be really boring!

I finally decided to stick to tried-and-tested attire and picked out a pair of grey bell-bottoms and a pink skivvy, matching pumps and earrings for my first day in school.

The door bell rang. I laid my clothes out on the bed and ran to open the door. It was Gary's batman. He handed me an invite and took his leave. The handwriting was bold, probably Pam's.

Lt. Col. Gary & Pam Randhawa

cordially invite

Maj. George & Eva Chandy

to

The Key Club Evening

on Saturday, 16/07/85

Venue: Block no. 49

R.S.V.P: 6549

I had heard of all sorts of parties and galas, but The Key Club was a first – and the invite was for that very evening. This was short notice.

I kept the invite on the dining table, turned on the radio and began preparing lunch. George came home at two. Saturday is a half day, so we had the afternoon to ourselves. We sat down to a leisurely lunch of chicken and rice, and George was telling me about his day when I remembered the invite.

I interrupted George and handed him the envelope.

'An invite from Gary? He didn't mention anything this morning.'

George pulled the invite out of the envelope.

His expression went from curious to shock to rage. He tore the card and threw the pieces in the dustbin. I went after him.

'I am assuming we aren't going for the party ... which is fine, but why are you so angry?'

'It's just one of those stupid parties where they drink themselves silly. And we have better things to do with our Saturday evening, don't we?'

'But what is The Key ...'

He pulled me close and kissed me.

'George, are you kissing me or trying to shut me up?'

'Neither, I am just having a very hard time resisting you.'

He picked me up and headed for the bedroom and all conversation was put on hold, indefinitely. His bare chest, the rippling muscles of his arms silenced me quite effectively. He stripped and I watched.

I like to watch. I am not sure if it's normal for women to be voyeurs. Maybe it's some kind of a psychological disorder. 'We'll just have to live with your voyeuristic slant,' George jokes. There's a full-length mirror opposite the bed. I see our bare bodies, entwined. George caresses my midriff and there is a certain rhythm to it which one almost misses in the haze of passion. But the mirror never lies. It shows that a man, if he really chooses to, can fulfill a woman and not merely fill her. Our bodies look beautiful together, his strong and sinewy thigh against my fair one. It's a heady feeling to watch myself being touched by his big, brown hands. The mirror fuels that hedonistic feeling as he lowers himself to kiss the tingling cave between my thighs. I feel naked.

It's not the absence of clothes that makes me feel naked; it's when the primal instinct surfaces, and I call out to him to make love to me, that I am completely naked in his arms, in body and mind. The eyes in that moment know no shame and it's only George's name that comes to my lips, again and again.

My first day at school was mostly uneventful, except for a disturbing piece of news from one of my young students. The children were dressed in neatly pressed uniforms – steel-grey pants and skirts and red blazers, badges with their names and handkerchiefs pinned to their chests. I spent some time getting to know their names.

'It's your turn, honey,' I said to a pretty girl in pig tails.

'Not honey, I am Bunny, and my dad is your husband's boss,' she said, haughtily.

Now, six year olds can be very smart, but such smugness comes from smart-mouth parents. Clearly, Bunny had heard either Col. Tehlan or his wife discuss my appointment as the new teacher, and whatever they had to say about me was not very pleasant. It was visible in the defiant tilt of Bunny's head.

I smiled at her and moved on to her companion, a shy, wheatish-complexioned girl. She stood up, fidgeted with her handkerchief and scratched her head. I encouraged her to speak, but the other children teased her with loud whispers of 'jun', lice.

She sat down without saying her name and Bunny pinched her arm.

I gave Bunny a stern look and asked her companion once again to tell me her name.

She began to cry and wet her pants. For a six year old, that can be very embarrassing. It looked like her peers had witnessed it before, because they started chanting, 'Shame, shame, poppy shame!'

Loudly and firmly, I asked the children to pipe down and threatened to make them all stand on one leg.

I took the little girl to the staff bathroom. Fortunately for me, another teacher met me on the way.

'Mrs Chandy, where are you taking Junaira?'

That's where the nickname 'Jun' had come from.

'I need to send her home, maybe speak to her mother.'

'She's out on rounds.'

'Her mother teaches here?'

'Oh, you don't know? She's the principal's daughter.'

Oh, my God, this was disastrous. I took a deep breath and told Junaira we were going to look for her mommy.

The principal, it would appear, had already heard of the incident for we met her midway. For some reason, I found myself apologizing. She gave me a brief nod and took Junaira with her.

Back in the classroom, the children were making so much noise I thought it might bring the roof down.

Once again, I screamed at them to settle down. They

took their places and I asked them to show me what they had done so far.

Their notebooks were poorly maintained, mostly in tatters. I asked them to bring new notebooks and leave these at home. At a loss for something to do, I asked them to draw me an apple and colour it with crayons.

The children were happy to oblige, except Bunny, who gave me what could be a child's version of a sarcastic look. Drawing apples didn't appeal to my husband's boss's daughter.

Welcome to school! I couldn't wait to get home, but telling George that was a big no-no; he would simply ask me to resign.

Somehow, I got through the day and the bell rang; the children rushed out of the class and I took a breather. Then I gathered my stuff – the fancy jacket, the cotton satchel and made my way out. Parents were waiting at the school gate to receive their children. Most fathers were on bicycles and probably harboured hopes of a better future for their children. Isn't that what school was about?

I knew that I had a long task ahead of me; teaching these children would not be easy.

As I walked out, I saw a moped pull in. A woman wearing a nurse's uniform got down. It was Wilhelmina.

'What a pleasant surprise!'

'Is there some place we can talk?' she asked a little nervously.

'Sure, let's go to my class.'

We chatted on the way but she seemed distracted.

When she was sure we were alone, she took out something from her pocket and gave it to me. It was an old pendant, probably made of silver. It had turned black in places, but was beautiful all the same.

'It's very pretty,' I told her, not knowing what else to say.

'Keep it. It's for you.'

'Oh, no, thank you. It's probably expensive.'

'No, it can't be very expensive. It's hers.'

'Who's her?'

'The woman ... I changed her clothes when you brought her in that evening and put it all aside, and then she died. We gave everything to the police, the clothes and the gold earrings. But the pendant got left behind in the locker. And later, when I looked at it, I didn't feel like returning it.'

'Wilhelmina, the police may be able to find her family because of the pendant! It's evidence.'

'No, this pendant has nothing on it that could be of use to the police. Go ahead, have a look.'

I turned it upside down. The chain was ordinary and so was the pendant, except for the delicately carved face of a tiger, but you had to look really closely to see the carving.

'Well, then just keep it, Wilhelmina. Maybe it'll bring you luck.'

'Sure, but I think it would be really selfish of me to keep it. She would have wanted you to have it, like a token. I had a dream about it last night. She asked me to give it to you.'

I was dumbfounded. She dreamt of the dead women and was here to give me the pendant at *her* request. It was all too freaky!

'No, Wilhelmina. Thank you but I can't take it. Just give it back to the police.'

'I can't ... It'll reflect poorly on me, my job at the hospital. Everyone will say the head nurse steals the dead patients' belongings. No way! I am leaving it. Here, take it! Keep it, throw it out, I don't care.'

The truth was finally out.

With that, she walked away. I called out her name, but she did not look back.

It felt strange, carrying the pendant home. It was like carrying a deadly secret.

Bunny

Bedtime Stories

'Stop screaming, Bunny! Papa is not going to be home for dinner. Finish your milk and go to bed.'

'I don't like milk and Papa always puts me to bed!'

'Bunny, he has gone to a party. He'll be late and you have school tomorrow. Drink or you'll get a tight slap from me.'

'No! I'll tell Papa you hit me!'

Mummy won't touch me. He'll get very angry with her if she does. I don't like Mummy, she's always shouting at us when Papa is not there. But when Papa is there, she doesn't say anything. Mummy is scared of Papa and Papa loves me.

Mini, my sister, is always sitting in Mummy's lap. I heard Pam Aunty say that Mini is a 'retard'. I asked Papa what the word means and he said that it means 'angel'. But Pam Aunty likes me more than Mini, I should be the bigger retard!

Mini can't talk or walk properly. Even Papa doesn't speak to her.

Sunny, my big brother, is scared of Papa. Papa scolds him a lot, but he got Sunny a bicycle on his birthday. I want to ride it too. Papa says he'll teach me next year, when I am bigger and stronger.

Papa calls me 'Papa's girl'.

I'll wait for him. Mummy is wrong, he'll come to kiss me goodnight. He always does.

The commandant's office is regal, all red carpet and carved wood. The brigadier is sitting on his swivel chair, asking his wife to get off the phone because he has people waiting in his office.

Poor Brig. Sargam is quite the dandy and has maintained himself well, while his wife is a round as a football and can be seen rolling down the hills of Jacob Hills as trying to lose all that fat. Some evenings he accompanies her. They make a Laurel-and-Hardy couple with him in a smart track suit, and her in an ugly printed sari.

He finally gets rid of her and addresses Col. Sampat of the Military Police. The brigadier is totally clueless about the death of the unknown woman. The local police aren't allowed to question the officers, so the army conducts its own inquiry. The colonel has driven down from the area headquarters in Shimla especially for this purpose.

The colonel apprises the brigadier about the murder and the suspicion that one of his boys could be involved. The word 'involved' raises the brigadier's hackles. He looks at me pointedly.

I don't have much to say in my defence except that I happened to be at the church at the right time. Their blank faces tell me they are not impressed and that I am well past the age of a boy scouting around deserted places.

True, I am a thirty-one-year-old bachelor who enjoys his own company. I do my job well, but it is not enough. The army requires me to have a wife, host dinners and drink like a fish to be a part of the social circus.

I do none of this. Hence I am the black sheep of Jacob Hall.

I sit quietly, hands folded, listening to both of them express spurious concern over the death of the woman. The brigadier is interested in hearing the gory details about the burn marks on her body. They call the man who left her there 'a dog' and discuss at length what it must have been like for the poor woman to be tortured so.

I nod; that's all that is expected of me. I quietly drink my tea, thinking of Friday evening when I had carried her in my arms. Her body was warm against mine and the blood had seeped slowly into my hands, my clothes and my head.

She was shivering in the blue sari, her body language said that she was sorry to have caused such inconvenience. The abused are always apologetic, as if somehow it's their fault that the abuser is punishing them.

There are days I feel like that too, weary, ready to give

up. It's been years since the disgraceful episode in Nagaland, yet I think of it every day.

I was newly commissioned and that was my first posting. I was deployed with twenty men under my command to the west of the hill ranges on the Indo–Burma border.

It was a time when Naga hostilities were at their peak. Our task was to prevent the movement of hostiles across the border. The commanding officer was reluctant to send an inexperienced officer on the mission, but being an overconfident youth, I managed to convince him to let me lead the men.

We began our journey before daybreak, at three in the morning. As we walked into the thick foliage through the tricky terrain, the humidity made us strip to our skins.

We stopped several times to remove leeches from our backs and necks. We would burn them with our cigarettes, and the ugly creatures, now fat from sucking all that blood, would fall to the ground. There was a sadistic pleasure the men derived from burning the leeches; sprinkling salt on them was another way to get rid of them, but nobody ever exercised that option. The thrill of burning and watching the leeches squirm made us forget our own discomfort.

An hour before nightfall, we started to set up camp near a river. We had barely finished when we heard a strange siren, which set the whole jungle humming. Birds flew out from the trees in all directions and suddenly there were arrows flying at us.

We were ambushed. Half of my men died on the spot; the poisoned arrows proved far deadlier than our bullets.

The rest of us ran for cover before opening fire in the direction from which the arrows came. This continued for a while. Then there was a loud thud and a body fell down a tree. We fired some more shots and walked over to where the body was.

A tribal wearing a loincloth and a belt of human skull and bones around his waist lay bleeding. The bullet had entered just above his pancreas. I could not leave him there to die, so I picked him up and took him back to the battalion.

We were able to save him, but that in no way dimmed the guilt of being responsible for losing ten lives. It was described as a heroic deed: 'An officer saves the life of a hostile tribal'. The army was made to look good, aiding the locals. The incident even got me a shiny medal.

The medal got my career going, but I didn't care a damn anymore. The truth was different from the fabricated story.

I used to be as carefree as any of these YOs, but all the rigorous training had not prepared me for that day in the jungle. In my inexperience, I had led my men to death. We never should have camped near the river. We were out in the open with no cover, exposed, and it was my mistake.

I should have treated the threat of the Naga hostiles more seriously. One ill-informed decision on my part had cost too many lives. I was answerable to the dead soldiers' families – the blind parents, the only son, the pregnant wife – different scenarios and all ugly as hell.

It's a heavy burden to carry, so many deaths and so many curses. My head aches from carrying it all for so long. There are days I wish somebody would just blow my head up into tiny pieces.

The only time I feel better is when I am in the classroom, teaching YOs the importance of training well. To know their job before they go into the field and get themselves or someone else killed.

At twenty-three, one is not afraid to die or kill. Your understanding of the environment is limited to playing a heroic role. There are lives at stake and men who depend on you to lead them back home – but these matters are far from the minds of these young men.

They are here simply to get grades that look good. Who has ever learnt from the experience of another? Everyone must face their own hell! They think heroic deeds will follow when the time comes. But the time comes unannounced, and mostly, when you are least prepared.

Brig. Sargam reaches the end of some story and Col. Sampat nods his head in agreement. We are all great storytellers in the army and have many stories to tell each other.

Meeting over, we take the brigadier's leave. I follow Col. Sampat out.

'Major, what were you doing at the abandoned church?' he asks me.

'I went there for some quiet time.'

'Quiet time? Are you out of your mind? Look at this place, it's quiet no matter which direction you walk in.'

'Well, that's the direction I took.'

His eyes, loaded with suspicion, probe my face.

Then he asks if I knew why the woman was barefoot and then answers his own question.

'Her being barefoot can mean two things: either the woman was brought there with the intention of being killed, or she came willingly. One of those loose women who just meet a bad end.'

That makes me angry; how quick people are to pass judgements.

'Colonel, she was no loose woman. She had to be an officer's wife.'

'What makes you say that and with such confidence?'

'She asked me to put her down and said, "The bloodstains won't easily wash off from your games uniform."'

I let that sink in. He knows I am right. A pair of white shorts and a white collared T-shirt is the standard games uniform in the army, but a civilian would probably not know that.

'An army officer's wife would have been missed. Jacob Hills is a small place.'

'Maybe some officer drove her down here from Shimla. For them it's just a short road trip, Colonel.'

'I checked the log for Friday and the day before at the main gate. The sentries have strict orders to record every entry and exit. Their records show no couple entering Jacob Hills on a bike or a vehicle, which can only mean that the woman was living here at the time of her death.'

'If she was living here then it should be very easy to find her killer.'

'There are about two or three hundred officers who come to Jacob Hills for their courses. Only permanently posted officers are allowed family accommodation and the temporary officers' accommodation is limited, so the majority comes sans family. It was a common occurrence in my time that, if an officer went on leave, he gave his home to a fellow officer to use it in his absence. The trend seems to have changed slightly in the last five or six years. The new breed of officers are fucking misers! They rent out their houses to other officers when they go on annual leave and make a little money on the side.'

Col. Sampat was right. It was a common practice indeed. Most officers did it for free, but there were those who didn't mind making an extra buck or two, unofficially.

'If she was staying with her husband in one of the rented houses, someone would have seen her.'

'Not necessarily, unless they were the socializing kind. And I don't think he could really risk taking her out the way she looked. What say, Major?'

I remember how she looked, like a broken doll with ugly scars. No, I don't want to be reminded of her.

She is dead, I am still alive.

The Dead Mona Lisa

'Push the curtains aside; let some light come in. Keep clicking.'

Images of the dead woman were displayed on the screen as the sergeant pressed the remote of the projector. The body had been lying in the morgue for two days. Since no one had come to claim it, we had no choice but to hand it over to the police in Shimla.

It wasn't a top priority for the local police, but the army authorities – mostly I – were insisting on a thorough post-mortem and not merely filling a paper announcing the cause and time of death.

Beyond that, my hands were tied. The unidentified and unclaimed body was to be cremated at government expense.

The procedure for cremating an unidentified body is quite hazy. For instance, during my previous tenure in Punjab, after Indira Gandhi's assassination, the security agencies secretly cremated bodies labelled unidentified.

These cremations were of people picked up by the police for interrogation about their links with the separatist movement. Rumours were rife that it was being viewed as a speedy means of weeding out the Sikh separatist militancy in Punjab.

Whatever little sympathy I had for the separatists being butchered in fake encounters with the police died down when I read a detailed Research and Analysis Wing (RAW) report on Operation Blue Star at the Golden Temple.

The army had found not just arms, ammunition, alcohol and a treasure trove of AK 47s in the holy place of the Sikhs, but also skeletons of young women, dozens of them piled in a room. It is said that no girl came out alive from the Golden Temple; the skeletons proved that to be true.

Women down the centuries have fascinated men to such an extent that they forget that certain things are taboo, like murder and rape.

If Maj. Alex was right, the dead woman was the wife of an army officer and, with the body gone, the clever bastard would be off the hook. The husband would simply go back home and explain to his parents and relatives that she had run away with another man, which was quite common these days.

A man who tortures and kills a woman, leaving her to die, must have ensured that no one ever saw her and, even if they did, she must have been dull and mousy enough to have gone unnoticed.

I wanted to do more, but that really wasn't my job. Brig. Sargam had made it very clear that his men had nothing to do with the dead woman, and that he didn't wish to see me in Jacob Hills asking a lot of questions. With so little to go on, it seemed unlikely that we would find the man responsible for her death.

Maj. Alex was an interesting element in the story, a confirmed bachelor. He had bumped into not one but two women on the same evening. He had not mentioned her, but the nursing staff at the hospital had told me the other woman was a Mrs Chandy, the wife of another instructor at PIT.

A bachelor found alone with a colleague's wife in an abandoned place spelt mischief.

I would run down to see her with the dead woman's photographs. It's easier to investigate with pictures of the dead; people are more open, and the lady here was no Mona Lisa in death. Despite the calm of death on her face, one look at the pictures would tell you she'd died horribly.

The autopsy report had been downright murky. The woman was being abused and tortured. It was evident from the burn marks made by cigarette stubs on her body. Her toes and fingers had been broken and joined several times. She had a hairline rib fracture and practically no strength or blood in her body.

Even before she died, she was in a pitiful state. Her death was just a formality.

The Tiller's Club

We took the spiral Burma teak staircase to the terrace and crossed the Italian marble floor. The huge paintings of old and withered British viceroys didn't seem to flatter the decor at night.

The Tiller's Club is over a hundred years old, and the British had spent lavishly on making the club a place befitting royalty. There was a beautiful palanquin with aquamarine stones and rubies in the foyer which I loved. A tall porcelain vase was kept near the entrance of the terrace, and a lush curtain creeper curled up the doorway. White cane sofas and tables were spread all over, and men and women chatted away in groups with drinks in their hands. Waiters in white fan-tailed hats and red cummerbunds ran about serving snacks and kebabs from the grill.

It was a really cold evening, but the women were dressed in sleeveless blouses and shimmering saris. I questioned my choice of clothes – red bell-bottoms with a black skivvy and a red scarf around the neck. George read my mind and smiled and whispered in my ear, 'It's better to be warm and cosy on a chilly November evening than be cold and stupid.'

George really said the most endearing things. I wanted to kiss him, but in a circle where air kissing branded a woman as fast, I resisted the urge.

We looked around for a free table, but since there weren't any, we headed for the bar. We had come for dinner, thinking a Wednesday night would be a quiet affair – but it appears there is nothing like a quiet evening at the Tiller's. Since all the chairs were occupied, we took the leather stools closest to the bar. It was a huge, all wood bar, and was being manned by two barmen.

There were well-oiled senior officers sporting long moustaches and pot-bellys at the bar, but no one familiar. They drank Old Monk, Salon No.1, smoked Gold Flake and talked loudly.

George ordered both of us a lime cordial with a dash of gin, and we relaxed into our stools. He chose to face the bar, while I looked on at the merry people occupying the cane sofas.

I saw a man walk towards us with a smile pasted on his face. It was Col. Tehlan, George's boss. A burly fellow, quite the happy-go-lucky type. The way he held the beer mug close to his chest and swayed, I could tell he had come to the club without his wife.

I muttered his name under my breath and heard George groan, 'Oh, no.'

'Mrs Chandy, how do you do, ji?' He had an appalling accent and kept falling into Punjabi when he couldn't find the right word in English.

'Very well, thank you, Colonel. Your daughter is very attentive in class.'

'Not enough, going by her marks in the class test.'

I tried to assure him that Bunny was an intelligent child and only needed a little guidance.

Col. Tehlan soon coaxed George into playing a game of billiards. As he spoke, a waiter switched on the lights in a room adjacent to the terrace and started arranging the colourful balls together.

From where I was, I could see George laughing loudly at something the colonel said. My husband became a different man around people, jovial and hearty. But that's true for all of us. We become different in a crowd, we laugh differently, talk differently.

I sat watching them. The colonel was good and my George is no player, but he was warming up to the game. One game turned into two and I ordered my second lime cordial.

There were different officers at the bar now, a younger lot drinking whisky on the rocks. They were drunk and sniggering about how good 'she' was. 'She' was standing at a distance with her back to me. She was painfully thin and her hip-bone jutted out of the red sari she wore. Her hair was in a back-combed bouffant. The officers looked her up and down and dissected her anatomy.

Soon, she turned to greet someone. I was surprised to see that her face was devoid of any remarkable feature and her insipid eyes didn't smile when her thin lips broke into a grin. The men continued to rave about the nondescript woman.

It was baffling. What were the men sniggering about? She had an S-shaped figure and she stooped when she walked. She must have felt my gaze, for she returned it evenly. I looked away as she joined the other couples.

George was still playing and a lot of loud guffaws on his part told me that he was winning too. I was a little angry at him for deserting me but he seemed so happy, the anger disappeared.

Just then Pam, chic as ever in a green maxi, joined me at the bar.

'Eva darling, what are you doing sitting at the bar alone? Where is the charmer?'

'George is over there playing billiards. I have just been nursing my drink and eavesdropping on these YOs.'

'Really? I didn't think you had it in you.'

'Pam, you'll be surprised what I am capable of,' I carried on in the same manner as her.

'What are they talking about? That they fancy you?'

'Don't be so fanciful, Pam! Look there, you see that thin woman in the red sari? They've been talking about her like she's some firecracker. I don't understand. She looks so ... ordinary.'

I was ashamed just for a second as the word 'ugly' popped in my head.

Pam gave me one of her enigmatic smiles and replied, 'She has a big mouth.'

'She can talk well, then?'

Pam almost fell down laughing, and in between gasps, she managed to say, 'No, if she started talking they would all run … She's known to give the best blow job around here.'

'Oh, that's terrible!'

'No, my dear, trust me, the men think quite differently,' she said, raising her finely arched eyebrow. She sounded almost jealous.

'Who is she?'

'She's the wife of Major Vikram Singh. He's with the administrative wing. He's a no-good fellow, a feral, highly ambitious sort. The story goes he pushed his wife to sleep with a pot-bellied colonel – I'm not saying who – a while back. There was a sudden rush to Delhi for a quick abortion, and when she came back, she took to sleeping around with a vengeance. It's almost like payback time and Vikram is made to look like a right royal fool.'

'But does she really have to do that to teach him a lesson?'

'At some party I heard a disgruntled Vikram tell her, "I told you to stick to officers in my course." And she's no innocent soul. I bet she enjoys it too … teaching him a lesson.' Pam winked at me and continued, 'So, she's never short of company. When one officer finishes with her, he passes her on to another. As you can see, her fame has gradually grown,' Pam finished on a note that bordered on envy.

I was so indignant, I could barely speak. This wasn't just dirty, it was against everything a woman stood for. I wasn't judging her. It didn't bother me that she did what she did, what bothered me were her reasons.

Pam said she had to go, they were waiting for her in the dining area. Before she left, I asked for the woman's name.

'Look at you, Eva, a regular gossipmonger, aren't you? Her name is Saryu.'

It was the name of a river in the Ramayana. I wondered where this namesake of the river was carrying all that dirt? Where was she headed? It had nothing to do with me, and I gradually put the odd conversation out of my mind, but I was no longer sure I liked the people in Jacob Hills. There were so many undercurrents – I didn't want George and myself to be swayed by them. Thank God, there were only eight more months and we would move out, safe and sound.

Time passed, and I began to devise a question paper for my students' quarterly tests. I had to ensure that most of them passed. They could spell A for apple, but A for aeroplane was another story.

The children were behaving themselves and Junaira was beginning to open up now that I separated her from Bunny.

That girl was positively bossy and Miss Chandy was just a glorified ayah to her.

I bore her tantrums as best as I could, but something about her behaviour bothered me.

I had noticed a day before, when the children were rushing to their respective guardians once school got over, Junaira said bye to Bunny and walked on to where her mother was discussing something with another teacher. The batman who came to pick up Bunny was late, and she stood there playing with her hair, impatiently awaiting her ride. Her older brother offered to take her home on his cycle, but she sent him away.

The jeep was waiting for me, so I offered to drop Bunny home.

She refused, saying she would only go home with her bhaiya. While it's normal for children to be attached to the batman as they spend a lot of time playing with them, Bunny is not your average, affectionate child.

Just then, the batman came on the cycle and Bunny rushed to embrace him. She went with him without a look in my direction. I didn't like her being so friendly with the batman, but I wasn't sure her mother would appreciate my advice.

Maybe I would tell her when I met her at the Husbands' Night.

I finished setting the question paper around mid-day. During the break, the peon led an officer in military uniform and a red beret to the classroom. He said, 'sahib was looking for you.'

Sahib had an impressive moustache and a very regal bearing. His gaze was piercing. Very formally, he introduced himself as Col. Sampat of the Military Police.

I just stared, hoping he would say something, but he returned my gaze with a neutral look and handed a bunch of pictures to me.

They were black-and-white mug shots of the dead lady, her skin scrubbed clean, eyes shut and face set in death.

I took a quick look and returned them to him.

'You along with Major Alex found her on the roof of the church?'

'Yes, we did.'

'What were you doing there?'

He didn't say it in so many words, but the tone of his voice implied, What were you doing there with Major Alex? It made me a little angry, but it was a valid question.

I told him about George's accident, his posting and that evening at the church. He seemed to visibly relax as I described the events of that evening and even smiled at me – a smile that he must reserve for ladies that deserve respect, I assumed.

Men are like that. They are quick to judge a woman as loose, based on little or no evidence. It helps them to undress her in the dark room of their mind without any guilt.

I kept a blank face and did not return his smile.

'You were with the woman when she died. Did she tell you who she was or who did that to her?'

'Nothing, no idea whatsoever.'

'What was your impression of her?'

'She didn't say much, just that she had no children. For some reason she was sad about that. From her accent, I gathered she was from the North, and had fallen for a man from the East, probably a Bengali.'

'What makes you say that?'

'She was humming a song in Bengali, but the accent wasn't right. It was as if she was repeating something she had gotten used to hearing.'

'We'll look out for a Bengali chap in the course.'

'You think an officer is involved in her death?'

'Yes, preliminary evidence suggests that she's an army officer's wife and had been living here at the time of her death.'

'Oh, then I am sure someone will know her!'

'I am afraid, Ma'am, we have had no luck with the pictures so far. The bastard probably kept her locked up.'

'Colonel, I don't think he would have had to lock her up. There was no fight in her. If he wanted her to stay indoors, that's exactly what she would have done.'

The colonel thanked me for my time and left.

I sat there checking notebooks and thinking of the silver pendant lying in my dressing table drawer. It had to be a gift. One didn't go about wearing old pieces of jewellery unless they were attached to them. Maybe he had gifted it to her during the early days of their marriage.

I decided that as soon as I got home, I would soak the pendant in vinegar overnight. It could be that the pendant was hiding a secret under all that muck.

I got up to stretch my limbs, cold from sitting indoors. I gathered the workbooks in my arms and headed to the field, where the sun shone nice and bright.

I joined Hemlata, the Hindi teacher, who was knitting a muffler for her brother, a soldier posted near the J&K border. She lived in the village and cycled up to Jacob Hills every day.

We chatted idly for some time before I went back to work. Suddenly I heard the sound of a child crying loudly. There was a cloud of dust as the children ran helter-skelter.

We rushed to the swing and found Junaira on the ground. Bunny said she had fallen from the swing, and went back to climbing the jungle gym. Hemlata picked her up and took her to the bathroom. She had wet herself again.

When Hemlata returned and resumed knitting, I asked her what was wrong with Junaira.

'The poor girl has been under severe trauma since the accident.'

'What accident?'

'Oh, it's more like an incident ...' she hesitated. 'Please don't tell anyone but Principal Madam tells everyone that it was an accident. She has been like this since she burnt her hand a month back.'

'How did her hand get burnt?'

'A man burnt her hand.'

'Oh, my God, who?'

'An officer ... He forcibly tried to kiss her on the mouth. And when she tried to run, he burnt her hand with his cigarette.'

'They didn't catch him, did they?'

'No, she had never seen him before.'

The bell rang and suddenly it was madness all around as children rushed to their respective classes.

I put my hand on Hemlata's arm and smiled to reassure her that this would remain between us.

In the classroom, the children were making paper planes and noisily talking to each other. A loud 'Good afternoon, Miss' sounded as I entered the class. They settled down to take out their pencils and rubbers from their pencil boxes.

I gave them dictation and walked around the benches, towering over them, checking the spellings. I scolded Bunny for drawing cartoons and not doing the exercise I had given her. Her homework was always incomplete. I remembered Col. Tehlan lamenting about it at the club.

I reached Junaira's bench and noticed she had put her pencil down. I picked up her workbook and saw that she had written all the spellings correctly.

She was a smart child, under all that quietness. I patted

her head and saw a shy smile break on her lips. I felt like hugging her and I did, which turned out to be a mistake, because she became agitated and started to cry loudly. In trying to console her, I became flustered and the other children cast accusing glances my way. Bunny, the obnoxious little thing, rolled her eyes as if to say, Miss Chandy has gone bonkers.

In time I managed to calm her down and took her hand in mine. It was then that I saw a round burn mark on the inside of her wrist. It was horribly similar to the grotesque chickenpox-like marks I had seen on the dead woman's stomach.

There couldn't be two men running around Jacob Hills burning women and little girls. It was the same man who had killed the woman. This man was no longer a figment of my imagination; he had a face. And Junaira had seen him.

Captain Rana

Fling-a-Ding

'Stop that, Heena.'

'Don't you like the foot massage?'

'I am feeling very ticklish today. Come we'll sit up and talk.'

The overcast sky outside matched the slyness in my heart. I had to break the news to Heena that I was going away for some time. It was a tough decision for me to leave her. I knew in my heart that I would miss her but she wanted to get married and at twenty-four, I am not sure I could handle the pressure of a job and marriage.

The biggest stumbling block was her religion. She was a Muslim and some of her relatives still lived in Pakistan. My parents would never agree.

Her burqa had been my pillow many times when we lay on the grass beside each other. I had taught her to kiss; a nineteen-year-old virgin has many inhibitions, but once the boundary is crossed there's no looking back. The burqa was put aside for good and now she dreamt of a wedding lehenga.

The senior officers are right when they say every woman has her unique scent, but the scent of the woman you love lingers above all.

I wish I had even a faint flicker of courage in me to prevent me from lying to her, and just simply saying, 'It's time I ran.'

This was not the first time I would be telling a girl the army needed its brave soldier back. These young girls are so clingy. A few kisses, a couple of nights together and they want to enslave you forever. Well, I wasn't about to give up my freedom so easily.

I gave her the news.

'Why didn't you say anything earlier?'

Because I was afraid you wouldn't sleep with me anymore – I could hardly say that to her, so the lies kept tumbling out.

'I got the transfer orders this afternoon. I don't want to leave you and go, Heena, but my job ... my country needs me.'

It sounded like a dialogue out of a Rajesh Khanna film, but it never failed to work. God, she was crying now, crying herself silly.

Women will never understand that tears don't become them and instead of melting a man's heart, they harden it so much that men can't wait to get away.

The time was five, still an hour to go before I dropped

her home. No, not home, but close by. She couldn't be seen riding home with a man sporting a crew cut.

'I'll write to you every day.'

Great, she was going to write to me every day, but where?

'I'll send you my address when I get there.'

'But where are you going, at least tell me that!'

'Oh, Heena, I wish I could. This is all highly sensitive information. I could be court-martialled for telling you.'

She buried her head in my chest and said, 'I'll wait for you to come and get me.'

'I'll be back some day. Would you like to go to the guesthouse again, before I leave on Monday morning?'

She nodded.

'What will you tell your Ammi?'

'That I am going to Mariam's place to study for an exam.'

The ride back to Jacob Hills was very quiet. I kept seeing her face. I felt guilty, but that never lasted long; I had learnt the art of wooing women from the finest.

Heena would wait a month, two, six maybe, and then put me down to a bastard and get married to a nice Muslim guy.

And who knows, perhaps I'll meet her in a market many years later, round and lovely, with half a dozen kids by her side.

The thought of her with another man wasn't really pleasant but what right did I have to be jealous if I wasn't going to be around to take care of her?

'It's all part of learning, my dear chap,' one of the Casanova regimental officers had once told me.

On the way, I made a detour to the Circuit House to book a room. It was difficult for the junior officers to book rooms at such short notice, but my charm worked well on men too.

I booked a room for Saturday night. I was going to make the most of our last time together. Whistling, I started my bike and rode into the mist that had settled on the road.

The Town Whore

It had all started two months ago. I was to go to Delhi for the abortion. It was really careless of me and Vikram was furious. He had said, 'I can't afford a baby right now, was a major's pay is two thousand rupees a month. Do I feed you or the baby? We have to get rid of it.'

Of course he wanted me to get rid of it. He didn't want to raise someone else's bastard. Vikram hadn't touched me in months. He did not desire me, but the colonel couldn't get enough. He visited our home every other afternoon, so it was no surprise that I was pregnant.

I gathered the courage to tell Vikram that I would not have an abortion. I thought he would shoot me with his rifle, but he said, calmly, 'Fine, then your lover can keep you and your baby.'

He called the colonel and gave him the news.

I heard the colonel bellow on the phone, 'What nonsense! I have nothing to do with her. She's your wife, your headache!'

'Maybe Saryu can say hello to your wife in Delhi when she goes for her abortion.' Vikram put the phone down and waited. Two minutes later, the phone rang and the colonel agreed to foot the bill for the abortion. He never wanted to see me again.

Strange are the ways of men. I remember the colonel looking deep into my eyes when he was on top of me and saying he would always be there for me. The word 'love' was tossed about as many times as he came, and afterwards he would say, 'You are the only woman who ever made me feel like this.'

I had believed him, believed that even though this had begun as a fling, he had come to feel for me. I even looked forward to his afternoon visits, and for those few months, we had been happy. And when I wanted to venture out of the bedroom with him, he humoured me. We went for short drives through the jungle. He even took me to the deserted church once.

We couldn't be seen together in public, but in private, he took me to many places. He talked of going to Kanyakumari and Goa with me, and soon those day dreams became my reasons to live.

He gifted me clothes, flowers and trinkets from the shops on Mall Road, and I slowly let down my guard.

He treated me like a lady and my ignorance made him laugh. I never knew what it was to love, but I was happy to be with him. His moustache didn't look so bad, nor did his love handles or his receding hairline. I had started to like everything about him.

Just when I was recovering from Vikram's brutal rejection, now the colonel too didn't want anything to do with me or his child.

Vikram pressed the receiver to my ears; he had seen the metamorphosis from hating the colonel's visits to pining for his company. He repeated the colonel's little speech verbatim.

'I have a wife and children. They depend on me and I can't let them down. I don't want to be involved in any kind of mess. She's your fucking responsibility, not mine.'

He had washed his hands of the whole thing just like that.

I didn't eat for two days and Vikram said, 'Good. We'll get rid of the rascal without the fuss and I can pocket the money.'

On the third day, I asked him to take me to the doctor.

Vikram put me on a train and asked his cousin brother in Delhi to take me to a doctor. I was scared. In the movies they always showed abortion as a blood bath, with sad music playing in the background. I survived the ordeal, the hospital smell, the knowing look of the attending nurse who thought I was an unwed mother posing as someone's wife.

The operation was simple, said the doctor, and there would be no pain. He was wrong, pain was all I felt. The pain of loss was overwhelming. I cried for hours. Next evening, Vikram's cousin took me to his house in Daryaganj and I was left to myself. The room had a single bed and, thankfully, a huge window. I looked outside.

A black phone sat on the dining table and rang very often. Each time it rang, it raised my hopes and dashed them again. Two days went by, but Vikram didn't call. I didn't know how to call him; one had to go through the army exchange to reach the home number. I didn't know any number. Vikram's cousin and his wife were pleasant people, but their patience was running out. Vikram hadn't booked me a return ticket. I had been staying with them for over a week now.

I had no money. They lent me some, reluctantly. His cousin dropped me at the old Delhi station, where the Himachal Express started. The station was overcrowded, yet one didn't feel safe in that crowd. I stood in a long queue to buy a sleeper class ticket. The train was running late by eight hours. I slept on the platform among the homeless, at home among strangers.

At Jacob Hills, I hitched a ride in one of the army trucks and reached home. Vikram opened the door and said, 'You should have called. What if I wasn't home?'

That night, over dinner, he casually mentioned that the colonel had got himself transferred and he now had a new boss. Vikram had invited him over the day after. I gave him a sharp look, which made him say, 'Protocol, darling.'

A month later, he showed me an invite.

He couldn't believe his luck. He had received an invite to one of The Key Club parties. Nobody knew exactly what went on in such gatherings, but the general impression was that some kind of orgy took place.

Vikram didn't think it necessary to take me along. What would the ugly village duckling do at a gathering of swans? He had dressed with care, even got himself a nice hair cut and a head massage.

Before leaving for the party, he told me, rather pleased with himself, that the new boss was very happy with his work. We both knew who was keeping the boss happy.

I was doing my duty by keeping my husband happy; on the side, I was making quite a few other men happy as well. Vikram didn't know or didn't care. As for me, I had come far from being a girl with complexes who hankered after her husband's love. I took whatever was offered to me.

The intrusion of my body no longer bothered me. At least they were nice to me in bed, and some even found me beautiful. I had learnt to enjoy the very thing I had hated once, my body.

That night Vikram came home early, drunk and rather vocal about the evening.

He had dressed smartly for the party and looked handsome. I had little doubt about him being the cynosure of all eyes. He had left with a curt, 'Lock the door and go to sleep.' I did, only to be woken up at one in the night.

'Get up and get out of my bed.'

His ego had been squashed to a pulp. The wife he was embarrassed to lug around was much sought after.

'Your presence was greatly missed. Everyone wondered why I didn't bring my "pretty" wife along.'

He spat out the word 'pretty'.

'Why didn't you?'

'I would have, had you told me you were screwing half of Jacob Hills, you bitch.'

I didn't flinch.

'I asked you to be close only to the colonel.'

Flushed, he could speak no more. The blood had rushed to his head.

'What, the pimp can't control the town whore anymore?' I said.

I didn't bother to hide the contempt in my eyes.

He wasn't jealous. Jealousy came out of love and there wasn't any between us. He didn't care about me. He just didn't want to look like a fool in front of other men.

He looked me from top to bottom, the dowdy cotton night dress, small breasts and hardened nipples and said, 'Maybe I should have taken you to the party, and who knows, in the bargain I would have got a real woman to bring home.'

I wanted to tell him that there are no real women, just as there are no real men.

The Pendant

Wilhelmina looked at me and away and then abruptly said, 'Okay, if it's for the best.'

'It is. They'll be able to find him.'

Wilhelmina disagreed with my decision to take the pendant to the Military Police, but I had no choice. I was sitting on potential dynamite.

She didn't offer me coffee, tea or conversation. It seemed like I had lost a friend.

The vinegar had worked its magic and the silver shone as it lay in my palm in the sunlight. I asked the army phone exchange to connect me to Col. Sampat of the Military Police when I reached home.

The operator couldn't place him immediately, and said he would find the number and ring back. I hoped he would call before George came home for lunch. I didn't want to tell him about the pendant. I intended to quietly hand it over to Col. Sampat, so it would be his headache from there on.

The phone rang a few minutes later; the operator said that the colonel was holding the line. He recognized me and instantly offered to come down to see me. I cooked up some excuse about being busy and asked him to come to the school in the evening. We were preparing for sports day, and the children would be doing their formation practice. He didn't ask why I wanted to meet him. We agreed to meet at five.

George came home for a quick lunch – they too had some inspection going on at the college. As we ate, I thought of telling him about the pendant, but then I would also have to tell him about Wilhelmina's little act. I kept mum, thinking that it would be out of my hand soon and so nobody needed to know about it.

All I intended to say to the colonel was that the lady had pressed the pendant into my hand. I didn't know if he'd believe me, but he could hardly accuse me of being a thief.

I left for school at four. All the children were dressed in white, and the first graders and the second graders were separated from the senior lot. After a few mock marble- and frog-races, they were left to play in the field.

I went back to the classroom. Col. Sampat walked in exactly at five. I could tell he was curious. I put the pendant on the table and explained how I had come by it. Of course, the questions followed.

'She gave you the pendant when you went to see her at the ICU?'

'It was in the pocket of my bell-bottoms. I found it last night. I had forgotten all about it.'

He rubbed it in places.

'It looks new and shiny ... Did you ...'

'Yes, I took the liberty of soaking it in vinegar overnight, and in the morning, I found this.'

A tiger head carved very delicately to show the tiger baring his teeth and just below it was the engraving:

Anita weds A.R.

1982

'This should help,' the colonel said after reading the inscription carefully.

'How?'

'Ma'am, the army keeps the personal records of all officers and their families, including marriage, birth of a child or death. It's a part of their service records. It's a tedious task, but we'll eventually find out how many Anitas and ARs married each other in the year 1982.'

'Well, there is this other thing. I am not sure if it would make sense, and I don't know if I should mention it at all ...'

'Everything you say to me will be treated as confidential.'

'Uh, the burn marks on the lady's stomach ... I think I saw something similar. You see, there is a child here who had a very strange encounter.'

I went on to narrate the incident that Hemlata had narrated to me.

The colonel seemed lost in thought.

'This could be a little tricky but, uh, can I meet the child?'

I thought quickly and asked him to follow me to the park. The principal and other teachers were at the far end of the ground. I led him to the swing where Bunny and Junaira were playing. I introduced him to the girls as 'uncle'.

Colonel Sampat knelt down to say hello to the girls. He lightly pulled Bunny's cheeks, and to my amazement, she threw her arms around him and asked him to pick her up and put her on the jungle gym. The colonel happily deposited her on the jungle gym, but Bunny wouldn't let go and asked him to lift her again.

I had noticed it on other occasions as well – that Bunny, despite being six years old, was always clinging to her father. He always carried her around, on all social occasions. Even when George and I had gone to their house for dinner, she was friendlier with George than with me and went and sat in his lap.

Colonel Sampat was totally enchanted by her and was gladly doing her bidding.

'What an affectionate child!'

I brought his attention back to Junaira, who had silently watched Bunny hogging all the attention, as always. In a stern voice, I asked Bunny to go and play, and put Junaira on the swing. Though the marks were easily visible, I didn't want to agitate Junaira by bringing them to her notice.

She sat on the swing and I instructed her to lift her hands and hold the chain. Colonel Sampat went and stood behind to push the swing gently and had a good look at the burn marks.

His grim face said it all.

I walked him to the main gate.

'Did the child tell you anything about this man?'

'I haven't tried to ask her. She is quite traumatized by the incident and I don't think her mother would appreciate ...'

'Yes, I understand, but see if you can strike a rapport. Children have amazing memories.'

I didn't wish to get involved any further, especially if it meant probing the child for information. As I was saying goodbye to the colonel, there was commotion in the background and I saw that all the children had gathered around the jungle gym.

I rushed back and found Bunny on the ground. Her knees were bleeding and her upper thighs were also grazed. I took her to the staff room and took out the medical kit to clean her wounds. I kept cleaning but the blood wouldn't cease to flow. Her tiny white skirt was all dirty and red.

I finally managed to bandage her knees. I thought she would need tetanus shots, so a trip to the hospital was necessary.

The jeep was outside, so I took a sullen Bunny to the hospital right away. She wasn't crying and neither was she asking for her mother. Strange child!

I asked for Wilhelmina as soon as I reached the hospital. They pointed to a board that read 'surgery'. We didn't need surgery, just a tetanus shot. But I really wanted to see her, tell her everything was all right and that I hadn't told the colonel anything.

'What's with you finding bleeding people?' It was Wilhelmina.

I was holding Bunny's hand and looked down to see that the bandage had stopped the flow of blood only for a while.

'Oh, she fell from the jungle gym and bruised her legs. She's Colonel Tehlan's daughter.'

Wilhelmina walked towards us, her gaze fixed on Bunny's knees.

'If she has hurt her knees, why aren't the knees bleeding?'

Wilhelmina lifted Bunny's skirt; underneath, her sky blue bloomers were also bloodied.

We both stared. Bunny tried to pull her skirt down. She pushed Wilhelmina away and ran out of the door. I ran after her, caught her in a firm grip and brought her back. Bunny was now wailing loudly and other patients started looking at us.

Wilhelmina met me half way and together we took her to the examination room. She put her on the bed and called another nurse to help. Wilhelmina then disappeared and came back with a young lady doctor.

'Your daughter?' She nodded in my direction.

'No, my student, she just fell ...'

'Wilhelmina told me. Just wait outside, Ma'am, and we'll call you.'

I wanted to stay. Examining a little girl is different from examining a woman. A child needed reassurance, but I doubted my presence would do that for Bunny anyway.

I hoped that she wasn't hurt very badly. It looked quite bad though, all that blood. I hadn't seen her falling, but the jungle gym is at a height, and maybe the angle at which she had fallen had something to do with the injury.

Twenty minutes later, the doctor walked out.

'Is she okay?'

'She's fine. We need to call her parents.'

Well, doctors are never very communicative. I went in to the examination. Bunny was in a blue hospital gown and looked quite pale. I went and brushed her hair away from her face. She gave me an angry look.

Wilhelmina came in and gave Bunny a Kismi toffee bar to chew. Bunny threw it away.

'Okay, if you are going to be difficult then I am going to give you the biggest injection we have.'

'My papa will come and kick you!'

'Your papa, young lady, is in for a shock. Never mind. You just stay here, and your parents will be here soon.'

'You called them?' I asked Wilhelmina as we walked out of the examination room.

'The doctor did.'

'Is it serious?'

'You tell me, is vaginal seepage in a child serious enough? At her age, she can have an infection, like say a urinary tract infection, but not vaginitis. She's been sexually active.'

I was shocked.

'Bunny is six, Wilhelmina.' I said, stunned.

'I am sure the bastard who plays with her knows that too.'

'You are saying it's a routine thing and not a one-off chance that someone may have taken advantage of her ...'

'It looks like the penetration has taken place frequently and the child is used to it. It could be anyone she's comfortable with or plays with.'

'That's ... that's absurd!'

'The doctor who did the check up figured that the child is used to being poked down there.'

Oh my God! Ugly things like this didn't happen to children of respectable families. They were protected from this kind of filth. And then I remembered how Bunny had thrown her arms around the batman. She had been very comfortable ... even eager to be with him.

I dreaded to think how Col. and Mrs Tehlan would feel. They came in shortly and rushed to see Bunny. She threw her arms around her father and began to sob, asking him to take her home.

Mrs Tehlan's face seemed to be carved out of stone. She offered no comfort to her little girl as she watched her husband fuss over Bunny. He seemed bewildered and most affected by the news.

I felt bad for Bunny, to have a cold fish like Mrs Tehlan for a mother – one who left her children's care to the batman.

Mrs Tehlan patted Bunny's head, but her gesture seemed devoid of emotion. Why was I being so critical of her? Probably because I wanted to choke her. I felt so angry. Why did women give birth if they couldn't keep their children safe? Bunny's understanding of sex, relationships and her surroundings would only become more warped with time if they didn't do anything about the situation.

I was worried for Bunny. Was this pseudo-modern couple capable of grasping the enormity of the situation?

'I am sorry about the whole situation, Mrs Tehlan. Perhaps you should question the batman who comes to pick her up. He's very friendly with her ...'

Col. Tehlan firmly but politely cut me short.

I understood, they were in shock and had no idea how to deal with something so horrible that had happened to their child.

They picked Bunny up and walked out.

Wilhelmina said after them, 'Typical of parents, outright denial. If you close your eyes, it didn't happen. Like an ostrich who buries his head in the sand and thinks all is hunky-dory.'

'What are we going to do about it?'

'What can we do? It's their child. They need to be careful who they let their child mingle with.'

She shrugged and left.

It was getting dark and I walked back home, my mind filled with thoughts.

The world had turned upside down, and where was George, my anchor? I wanted to discuss with him Bunny's peculiar behaviour. Both Bunny and Junaira had been molested, but while Junaira had retreated into a shell, Bunny had lost none of her exuberance. Junaira was petrified of a stranger's touch, but Bunny thrived on it.

I remembered how easily she had asked Col. Sampat to lift her up, or how she sat in George's lap playing with his tie. A child who's being molested would show signs of losing confidence, agitation and fear of people. Bunny didn't. There was something terribly wrong here. Bunny had been sexually violated, but she didn't fit the abuse pattern.

Bunny wasn't a scared child. She was defiant and playful, and that was an anomaly.

The light in the study was on, thank God!

The main door was not latched and I let myself in. George was playing the drums to Phil Collins's *'I Don't Care Any More'*. George always played with an anger and intensity that surprised his family and friends. He was known to be a mild-mannered man.

He struck the last beat beautifully, and I clapped with enthusiasm.

'I value a kiss over applause any day.'

I threw myself into his arms and the little stool creaked under our combined weight. The kiss was deep and wet and went on for an eternity. That's the thing about kisses. They don't let you break away. Like divers who surface to breathe and then lose themselves again in the depths of the vast ocean, George and I searched for that unknown treasure. His tongue in my mouth made me want him even more.

But the poetry of our kiss was cut short by the shrill telephone ringing in the other room. We ignored it the first time, but it rang again. I slid off George's lap. He kissed the nape of my neck before making a dash for the phone.

I changed into pyjama bottoms and a very old sweater from my school days. It was the colour of wine, threadbare and very warm. George hated it and said I looked like a street urchin in it. He joked that someday someone would mistake me for the maid and that he intended to throw it away before that happens.

'If anything ever happens to this sweater, I promise, George, you'll have to buy a whole new wardrobe for yourself because I'll burn everything you own.'

George usually doesn't take anything I say seriously. But there was this one time when we had a fight and he threw an expensive vase that belonged to me on the floor. I was so angry I burnt his favourite pair of trousers the next day. George was always saying how difficult it was for the 'goddamn' fauji tailor to stitch a well-fitted pair of trousers and this particular black pair he guarded with his life; he even ironed it himself.

It was a fitting revenge that set the tone in the house that nobody messes with my things. We laugh about it now, but it wasn't very funny then. George had come home from office and twisted his nose in disgust.

'What's the burning smell?'

I wasn't speaking to him, so I pointed towards the back door. When he saw what was burning, he freaked out. He didn't speak to me for two days. In the end, I had to jiggle a hip and seduce him out of his black mood.

I was still smiling, remembering that time, when George came in.

'Don't you think you should warn your husband about another exciting evening at the hospital?'

'Who was that on the phone?'

'Eva, honey, you can't go around telling people how to take care of their children.'

'What exactly did you hear, George?'

'That Bunny fell from the jungle gym and you took her to the hospital, where the doctor said she had some kind of infection, UTI.

'Vaginitis.'

'What's the difference?'

'A big difference, George! It's not some harmless infection; Bunny has been sexually abused.'

'The colonel is distraught and worried that this sort of talk will spread all kinds of ugly rumours.'

'Distraught, my foot! Their daughter's whole life may be ruined and they are worried about what people are going to think? They are insane!' I breathed out my frustration and looked at George.

'Quote "Vaginitis happens due to sexual contact, in case a woman has intercourse with a new partner or has multiple sexual partners" unquote, Head Nurse Wilhelmina D'Souza.'

'Oh my God, Eva!'

'Yes. And the colonel and Mrs Moron just walked out with Bunny, dismissing the whole thing as an infection.'

'You could be wrong about the batman. Usually the chap in the house is a trusted fellow.'

'George, these days you can't trust your own mother ...' I remembered Mrs Tehlan's phony concern.

George became silent for a while and then said, 'Eva, I'm not sure ... What can we do if the parents are being so obstinate?'

'George, please go see the colonel and tell him there has to be an insider involved. Someone Bunny trusts, otherwise she would have been traumatized. I think the poor child doesn't even know that what's happening to her is wrong.'

George poured himself a whisky and sat down to listen to me pouring out my anxiety.

'Even in the playroom, her gestures are inappropriate. She's always getting on top of a boy, asking him to become her pony.'

'At that age, children love a ride. They don't distinguish between a girl and a boy, Eva.'

'George, do you remember the dinner at the colonel's place, how Bunny sat in your lap? You didn't ask her to, did you? You are not fond of children and you could hardly ask her to get off in front of her parents.'

'So, the child took a fancy to me ...'

'That's exactly what I am saying, George. Bunny takes a fancy to men, but not women. She knows how to wrap them around her little finger.'

'Eva, that's nonsense! She's just a child!'

'A very knowing child, George. She's at a very impressionable age. Whatever a child knows, she learns from somewhere. My question is, who's teaching her?'

Heena

The Runaway Soldier

'What is your relationship with him? You were with him yesterday, and the day before that. Yesterday you were with him long after night fall!'

'We walked far.'

'You were with him for six hours! Tell me the truth!' Ammi shrieked. 'I am going to ask him what he was doing with you, all alone; wherever it is that you two were hiding.'

'I am not even going to answer that!'

'Allah alone knows how many men you have been sleeping with.'

'Ammi, I call him chacha-jaan. He's like my father!'

'He's old enough to be your father, but he's *not* your father, Heena.'

'Ammi, don't you feel ashamed saying such things about the man you love?'

'Why should I feel ashamed? I am not the one who's pregnant.'

Mother's scorn hit me like a slap on the face. I feared that any minute she would get up from the bed and beat me like she used to when I was a little girl. Of course, she was too frail to lift her hand at me, but her words were like the fire that must burn in hell to dry our souls.

Dozakh, hell, I knew, is on earth.

As anger fell away and the river of my tears died down, I thought hard about the circumstances that led a mother to be jealous of her daughter.

Ammi had led a tough life. Abba never earned enough to give her any comforts. She worked hard along with him and her needle brought in more money than he ever did. One day, he died of smoking too much chillum, leaving Ammi and her four children without a roof over their heads.

After Abba's funeral, we didn't see much of our relatives, but an old friend of Abba's helped her find a place to stay and work for her in the garment business. Imran chacha was a blessing from heaven in more ways than one – he liked Ammi and slowly something began to blossom between them. He was very fond of me and would often take me around the market on his broad shoulders. I wished he would become my new Abba.

Although he was wealthy, he had a wife and half a dozen children, and thus, no means of taking on more responsibility. The romance never developed into anything more concrete.

He stopped coming; we didn't see him for ten years. Ammi sent us to school, and one by one, my brothers went to the big city to work. Ammi and I lived alone. Recently, we heard that Imran chacha had become a widower and had moved back to his old house. He began to visit frequently. I would find Ammi fussing over him, when I returned from college.

They spoke of the old times, and joked about how he had seen her running down the street barefoot in her youth. They shared shy glances; so much had changed and so had they. Sometimes I could sense Imran chacha's annoyance with Ammi for cribbing about all her misfortunes, and the toll these had taken on her eyes, her health, and her many aches and pains.

He had no such grievances in life and every sentence he uttered ended in shukrana. I wished Ammi would learn from him, but anger had settled in deep. Every time she spoke, bitterness rose like the high tide.

I enjoyed Imran chacha's company immensely. For us the in-between years didn't exist. I was a little girl again and he reeled me in with stories of the divine, the Quran and the old pir-fakirs. I was so in awe of him.

One day, a dashing captain came along and stole me from the quiet life I had been living. The lure of an exciting life was strong and I found myself taking all the shortcuts that I had never taken in life, such as lying to my mother, missing college, and most of all, letting a man see me without my burqa.

As time passed, Ammi's nagging stopped bothering me, books didn't interest me and neither did Imran chacha's stories.

I was in love.

I let love steer him into my arms, into my heart and finally into my womb.

I had been pregnant for over a month. Ammi confirmed it for me – the morning sickness had left her in no doubt. She was desperate to marry me off to the wretched man with whom I had sinned. I was desperate too. I hadn't heard from him.

I had told him over and over again that Mariam had a phone. He could ring her place and leave a message. He hadn't written or called and, as my stomach grew bigger, my heart contracted.

I needed a husband. In a few weeks I would be unable to hide it from the world. I had prayed patiently, implored, begged and even bribed Allah to make him come to me.

I had waited long enough. Now I needed to find him and, in my desperation to find him, I had confided in Imran chacha. He had a friend, who was a sergeant major (JCO) at the Shimla cantonment, and we had gone across to see him yesterday.

Chacha's friend was a nice man who sympathized with my situation and told me very bluntly that it was very common for faujis to take naive girls out. When the girl or her parents demanded marriage, they disappeared faster than the last bus leaving town. He had seen many such cases in his career of twenty years.

He made enquiries and found out that no one by the name of Captain Rana was posted in any of the regiments in the last one year, so getting a forwarding address was out of the question.

I came home dejected. Ammi had been stewing the whole evening – where had I gone with her precious Imran chacha? In a fit of jealous rage, she accused me of having relations with him too.

I should have seen it coming when she told me sharply to change my kurti before I left with Imran chacha. It had a nice, flattering 'V' neck, and I had been wearing it all summer. Ammi had never before found it 'vulgar'.

'He doesn't come to see me any more. It's only you who interests him.'

I wanted to tell her that he would take an interest in her, if only she managed to look beyond the grim realities of life and spoke of anything other than how difficult life was.

She's a loving woman and a good mother, and I couldn't hold her deep-seated insecurities against her. For years she had come home weary from a long day's work and attended to our needs. In the night, she had retired to a cold bed with no arms to offer comfort or ears to hear her woes. As children, we would sometimes hear her stifled sobs. In time, the tears dried and a bitter woman was born.

I was scared of what the future held for an unwedded pregnant girl whose own mother was jealous of her.

She had called me behaya, characterless, with such conviction that for a long time I wondered if I had indeed seen Imran chacha as a way out of my problem. He was a widower, after all.

Such ugliness rose and fell with her words that when I closed my eyes, I saw a stream of blood running down my wrist. The man I loved had left me without a word, and now my mother had abandoned me too.

I had nothing to offer to the life that throbbed in my belly except shame.

Not the shame of falling in the eyes of the woman who gave birth to me, or the men who'll soon label me a whore, but the shame of facing Allah's pakh world, of falling in my eyes.

If my own mother could turn against me, the world would eat me alive.

A week passed and a strange thing happened. I walked past a tailor's shop that I had visited with him once. I walked past it again the next day, not sure if I really wanted to go in and lay bare his lies.

I couldn't believe that he would deceive me. He had held me close before he left as if he didn't want to let go of me.

No, I told myself. A month was a very short time for a soldier to settle down in a new place, and he couldn't have known what I was going through in his absence. Could he?

There had to be some explanation. He wasn't a coward.

I had to be strong or they would all come and spit on me,

like my mother had. Nineteen wasn't as young as I was made to believe. I was going to be a mother soon, and if nature thought me fit to be responsible for another life, I had to be ready for that responsibility.

But first, I had to find the father of my child.

Brig. Sargam

Man to Slaughter

'What kind of fucking idiots are they recruiting nowadays, Tehlan?'

Tehlan sat ramrod straight in the chair with an apologetic expression on his face while the YO stood at attention.

'Don't feel sorry for him, Tehlan. This idiot is the one who should be sorry. Bloody fucker has got us in a mess that could have been easily avoided.'

I was angry but one can't blame young men for sowing wild oats. I only wish the fucker had been a bit careful.

'Look here, young man. We have all been there, but you are not supposed to get caught with your pants down and your rear exposed.'

'Sorry, sir.'

'Being sorry is not going to save anyone's ass here. You fool, how are we going to send you to spy on another country when a pregnant woman can trace your whereabouts? A fucking tailor master ... I can't believe your luck.'

Flipping through the record of the young idiot, I found he had done well so far and even got Delta in places. God knows, the army needed smart men. It was too full of officers like Tehlan, who were no better than literate clerks growing fat on government salary.

Right then, Tehlan looked like a well-fed bull. The good life he led in Jacob Hills was beginning to show on his face – the free liquor and the free rations.

I looked at Rana. He was scared, I could tell, but it didn't show on his face. He would go far someday.

'All right, Rana. The wedding is on Sunday, and you are invited. If your parents can make it, well and good, otherwise we are all family here.'

I saw the mutinous expression in his pahadi eyes. I pushed the file away and stood up to face him.

'Look, son, this is the best I can do. Your paramour, is that how it's pronounced, Tehlan?'

'Yes, sir.'

'Your paramour left me no choice. Her uncle knows some JCO who has taken the matter up with the Colonel Adm (Administration) in Shimla and he has taken it even higher up. So either we court-martial you for conduct not befitting an officer, or you marry the girl, settle down, have the kid and sort it all out.'

He still didn't say anything. At that age, giving up your freedom isn't easy.

'Look, young man, the whole fucking world does it. It's

just your rotten luck that you got stuck for life with the first girl you screwed.'

The bastard stood there glaring at me with those beady eyes until he finally gathered the courage to speak.

'Sir, my parents have plans for me. I am the only son.'

'Oh, is that so? Well, I bet the girl's parents had plans for her too – one that didn't involve her getting pregnant by some passing cad.'

That was good Sargam, I thought to myself and smiled, but the young bugger looked crestfallen.

'So soldier, ready to take the plunge?'

'Sir.'

Tehlan nudged him and he said a very constipated 'thank you', but that was all right. The poor boy was headed for slaughter. It called for a little pep talk.

'Trust me, son. The baby will keep her busy. Soon she'll grow comfortably fat and you can live your life as you please.' I sighed, remembering breakfast with my wife.

She sat in her silk nightgown hogging buttered toasts, mixed fruit jam and a golden fried omelette on a side plate. Chanda, the housemaid, rushed in and out of the kitchen, her lithe frame wrapped in a tatty cotton sari and a blouse with nothing on underneath.

Oh, how my heart pounded for her.

'It's a good trade-off, Rana. Better than being sent home in disgrace over a piece of ass.'

'Yes, sir.'

I dismissed him with, 'Take care that we don't have to come looking for you on Sunday, or I'll have you hung naked, upside down.'

A mix of emotions passed on his face, and the most prominent was indignation at the apparent injustice of his rushed marriage.

After Rana left, Tehlan uttered a few incoherent words. The only thing that caught my attention was that the ladies had started rehearsing for Husbands' Night. It would be the usual boring song-and-dance routine, but it'd be nice to see pretty young wives rather than the round face of my grossly overweight wife.

Heena

Kacche Bhature

I replaced the old bed sheet, pillow cases and bedcover. We had married in a simple ceremony at a temple. His grim face as he placed the garland around my neck made me anxious, but at heart I was happier than I had ever been. I was getting married to the man I loved.

My dearest wish was fulfilled, even if it was in this roundabout way. They gave us a one bedroom-hall-kitchen accommodation to stay in. I was ecstatic.

I settled in quickly with my meagre possessions; he even took me shopping. Things weren't all okay. He was still angry about the manner in which I had come looking for him. I tried my best to draw him out, to get him to share his worries with me, but he came back from college only in the evening and would sit down to study again after dinner.

I had a house to run and food to cook, but I was very lonely. He didn't take me out that often, saying his course mates laughed at him for taking his wife out in a burqa.

Eventually, he asked me to stop wearing the 'ghastly' black costume. The gentry here was different from the butcher's lane where I used to live.

At times his words really hurt me. He had never spoken to me like that during our courtship. Now, nothing I said or did was good enough for him.

Even my reading the namaaz five times a day irked him. I found it strange that he prayed only once in the morning, provided he was not running late – and he was late every other day.

My bump was beginning to show, not that it mattered; everyone knew why he had married me.

Ammi was happy. She was beginning to let go of her old beliefs and learning to lean on Imran chacha again. A man can make such a difference to a woman if he chooses to patiently understand her fears, hold her hand and walk her through the worst.

But in my short life, I had come to believe that when you had one thing, the other ran out, and when you chased the other, something else slid away. When I was sleeping with Rana, I wanted to get married and run his house. Now that I was married and had a home, the love had run out. The magical nights when I had lain on bed holding on to every word he said, now seemed like a memory from another time. I wish I could trade this time for the one spent on the grass, under the blue sky staring at the stars. That carefree time when I knew nothing of pretence and hurt and heartbreak; life was a flowing river, meandering through narrow places but never stopping. But I was stagnating now, like water in a pool full of muck breeding tadpoles. One thing was certain: if he ever came to love me again, something else would go sour. There is always a big 'if' that keeps following us throughout our lives.

As I looked back over the past two months, I realized that I had lived a lifetime while waiting for him. I was disillusioned with life now but not in the same way as when I had stared at the cough syrup bottle and the sleeping pills near my bed. Those days of wanting to kill myself were in the past. This was a new kind of disenchantment, which told me that life was a cheat.

Allah's creation was self-destructive.

Seeing the dread in my eyes, Imran chacha would bring me books to read, books that spoke of a world beyond what we could see. I only saw darkness.

Ammi and Imran chacha had visited me twice so far and were happy to see that I had a kitchen up and running. Rana wasn't very tolerant of them and asked me to invite them only when he was out.

He was out often. His new responsibilities didn't keep him from catching up for a drink with his course mates. I missed the rapport we had once shared, and longed for things to return to normal.

I picked up the old bedcover and sat down to wash it. A strange thought came to me, I wish I could shake this man and tell him that it was he who had chosen this bedcover off the rack, had slept on it, felt it, let go his fears and found comfort in it. Yet, how quick he had been to discard it when he no longer needed it.

I wish people were like old bedcovers, who didn't mind being used and put aside. But this bedcover did. It wanted to be felt, touched and caressed like it once had been.

I smiled at my silliness and got up slowly from the stool. The doctor had advised against any kind of strenuous activity. The next visit was a day away. I had marked it on the calendar. The doctor had asked me to take special care of my diet, which reminded me that I needed to buy some fruit. The fruit that came in the ration shops wasn't of good quality, but the meat and eggs were fresh.

Rana's pay was only twelve hundred rupees a month, and most of it was spent paying off his Mess bills. The liquor was subsidized; a large peg of Hercules whisky and Sea Pirates rum cost only two rupees, but he still managed to run up bills of over a thousand rupees. He gave me two hundred rupees to run the house. It was difficult, but Ammi had managed in less. With the free rations that the army issued, we ate like kings.

It's a very comfortable life. They give you a house to stay in, food to eat, send you to new places where there are always new people to meet. Ammi said I was lucky to find myself such a match. Was I lucky? And if I were, why didn't I feel good?

I felt as lonely as before. The only difference was that now, instead of the walls, I could talk to my womb.

I showered and got dressed. I didn't have many pretty clothes like the other wives, but my youth carried me through. I wore a white churidar with a short pink kurti and hid my stomach behind the dupatta. I had been married two weeks, but I was two months pregnant.

I was to attend a rehearsal for some event they called the Husbands' Night. Eva Chandy was coming to pick me up.

They had come to the house to ask how I was doing. Rana had said, 'It's not a social call. They probably want to find out if I am beating you black and blue. Watch your mouth around them.'

Three of them came to visit, led by Mrs Sargam, the commandant's wife. She had a round face and had tied her hair in a lose bun. She wore a cotton sari with a blouse cut very deep at the back. The fat on her stomach and back fell out of the blouse in folds. Rana called them tyres.

She walked into the house followed by two younger women, one a Sardarni and the other a firang. They introduced themselves as Pam and Eva. Mrs Sargam sat like royalty and turned up her nose at the tea served in the chipped china Rana had at home.

I could tell by the way she kept glancing at my stomach that Mrs Sargam didn't think much of me. A low-class girl who slept with a dashing, young officer, got pregnant and became an officer's wife.

The counselling session on how an army officer's wife should conduct herself lasted an hour, punctuated with sympathetic glances from the other two women.

Rana came home early that day and grilled me on what the commandant's wife had said.

'You two should take it easy in bed till the baby is born,' she had told me and I repeated it to Rana.

'I am sure the old buffalo has forgotten what it's like. You know, the commandant is screwing the ayah?' He guffawed.

I just looked at him.

'What's that hurt puppy look for?'

'Will that be our future, too? I, an old buffalo and you, the stud bull screwing the maid?'

'Probably,' he said callously.

I didn't burst into tears or call him names. Why give a man the satisfaction of seeing you break when he doesn't care a damn? All the tears on this earth can't move a man who doesn't love you. Another lesson learnt the hard way.

I went into the kitchen and started chopping onions. He came after me.

'So, you have no problems if I fooled around?'

'I am legally married to you, and you have to support the baby and me. I intend to resume my studies once he's born. I'll start working eventually, and when I am earning enough, I'll divorce you.'

'You'll divorce me, but I ... uh thought ... you love me,' he stammered.

The onions stung my eyes, but I didn't want to cry. I wasn't going to be weak or beg. I had begged enough. Begged God, begged him. Nobody likes to give alms to a beggar, nor even a kind word.

'Just because I got pregnant doesn't mean I have to spend the rest of my life with the first man I slept with. Make all the plans you like. I just want my baby to be comfortable.' I looked him in the eye.

He didn't say anything, but his sarcastic smile said it all, he didn't believe me.

'If you don't want me in your life, I don't want you either,' I said.

Brave words! I hoped when the time came to say goodbye, I would be strong enough to take care of my child. I wanted his love, not his charity. I wasn't excess baggage. I was worth more, much more.

The jeep honked twice. I locked the door and put the key in my handbag. It was new, Ammi had given it to me because she said I would need it. I needed a lot of things, but most of all, I needed a friend.

The driver honked again. I warily said hello to Eva Chandy, envious of how classy she looked in dark-green bell-bottoms and a black jersey. My clothes seemed too bright with the silver sequins I had sewn all over the pink kurti and the dupatta.

I felt overdressed and uncomfortable. I wanted to run

back home and lock myself in. She didn't give me a chance and asked me to get in; we were getting late.

'Mrs Sargam will throw a fit if we reach after her. She's a regular Hitler, my dear. We don't want to hear one of her lectures on the importance of punctuality. I rather dread her wrath.'

I was enthralled by how natural she was, and promptly forgot my resolution to measure my responses. We chatted for the next five minutes, until the jeep stopped in front of another block. The driver honked and Pam came running down the stairs in a figure-hugging yellow kurti with a Patiala salwar minus the dupatta. She wore black sunglasses and bright red lipstick. I could smell her perfume from a mile away.

She got into the jeep, exclaiming that we both looked lovely. Pam seemed friendly too. She asked me a couple of questions, but before I could reply, she was already onto something else. She wasn't really interested in me, only in creating an impression.

I turned to look outside. We crossed a board that read 'Equitation Training'. I was perplexed. I didn't know what that word meant. But as I looked at the paddock and the wooden jumps, I realized it had to do with horses. Sure enough, we crossed the stables next and there were fine Arabian horses. I had sat on a pony when I was younger and the experience had been memorable.

Seeing me smile, Eva said, 'George and I used to ride very often. I miss that.'

'Really, Eva, I had no idea that George rode. Gary is a national-level jumper. I know a little too, we should get together,' Pam piped in.

'Not for a few months. The leg is getting stronger, but no point in taking unnecessary risks.'

'Eva, George is fit as a horse.'

The words were innocuous, but something in Pam's manner suggested that the remark wasn't as harmless as it seemed. Eva seemed oblivious to it, but I caught the faint undertone of envy. Ammi was right. If one is really listening, reading people and situations was not difficult. Had I paid attention to Rana's words, I would have seen through the farce. But in love one is not only blind, but hard of hearing as well. I leant back and closed my eyes.

Minutes later, the jeep stopped in front of a grand building with a beautiful rectangular lawn, much like a garden in a princely estate. There were dahlias in full bloom, dog flowers and marigolds swaying gently with the wind. In the centre, the most exquisite red roses stood cordoned off by white bricks mounted sideways.

The heel of my sandal went in a couple of inches as I stepped on the soft grass.

The glass pieces on the multi-coloured garden umbrellas shone in the sun and smart women in sunglasses and high bouffants chatted away under the umbrella. About fifty-odd chairs were laid out in six rows and were all occupied.

An elegantly dressed woman in a printed sari greeted

Pam loudly and asked her to quickly get behind the stage. The stage was much like an open-air picture hall with a wide wall and an elevated space in the front. Eva introduced me to a few curious ladies and the knowing look in their eyes made me shrink.

Sensing my discomfort, Eva suggested we grab a chair closer to the stage so we could watch Pam dance. We had just sat down when a black Ambassador pulled in and the women stood up, and someone murmured, 'Shhh, football's here.'

Eva pulled me to my feet too. We watched Mrs Sargam being presented with a bouquet and something in a shiny wrapper, which she asked the driver to put in the car. She was then escorted by Mrs Tehlan to the maroon sofa in front.

Mrs Sargam was clad in another of those chiffon saris that leave little to the imagination. The deep neck of the blouse gave a generous view of her cleavage through the pallu of the sari.

She walked in, rolling her ample behind and a collective, 'Good morning, Mrs Sargam,' went up.

She smiled and spoke to the ladies sitting closest to her. Tea was served and Mrs Sargam admonished the waiter for serving oversweet tea. The poor fellow almost dropped the tray and rushed back to get her a fresh pot of tea.

After tea, Mrs Sargam was escorted to the table where large borosil dishes were packed with chutney sandwiches, vegetable pakodas, hot jalebi and chhole. She surveyed the table and smiled, and Mrs Tehlan gave her the plate with great servility. Mrs Sargam turned and invited the other ladies to join in.

We filled our plates and munched on the golden fried pakodas and sandwiches. After finishing the small eats, Eva went to get us bhature, but the waiter hadn't got any so far – even Mrs Sargam was waiting for them impatiently.

Mrs Tehlan asked a junior officer's wife to find out what was taking so long. She hurried to the kitchen, came back and reported that the gas cylinder had run out and they were just changing it.

Another ten minutes passed and the first batch of bhature came. I eyed them greedily, but they disappeared into the plates of the senior ladies. I walked to the table to pick up a jalebi, and just as I was about to bite into it, Mrs Sargam shouted, 'You keep me waiting for twenty minutes and then you serve me kacche bhature!'

With that she threw her plate on the grass with such force that the sandwich and the pakodas went flying. The chutney splattered all over and we were all stunned into silence. I closed my eyes and opened them again, not able to believe that she had actually thrown her plate because of an undercooked bhatura.

The poor waiter froze and then quickly bent down to pick up the broken china and the fallen food items. She went and stood practically on his head and asked him the reason for the undercooked bhature. He stammered, 'memsahib, tel garam nahin tha.'

She dismissed the waiter, calling him a 'cartoon'.

Mrs Sargam then turned her fiery gaze on Mrs Tehlan and told her that the arrangements were in very poor taste. 'You should have taken more interest in organizing the evening, Mrs Tehlan. Very poor management, I must say.'

Mrs Tehlan seemed close to tears, but somehow managed to maintain a brave face.

Mrs Sargam walked back to her sofa, followed by Mrs Tehlan and the other ladies. Now Eva and I were the only ones still holding our plates. I was very hungry and grabbed the bhatura that had miraculously arrived on the table. Mrs Sargam stared at us and summoned Eva to her with the wave of a hand.

Eva wished Mrs Tehlan and enquired after her daughter. Mrs Tehlan fidgeted with her parandi and said a curt, 'Bunny's all right.'

Mrs Sargam patted the place on the sofa next to her. Eva sat on the edge and everyone watched her nod in agreement.

Lucky Eva, I thought. Mrs Sargam seemed to favour her.

After ten minutes, Eva went on stage.

Eva was to be the impromptu MC. She began by introducing herself and called for the first item on the programme: a mime by three ladies, acting as a husband, a wife and the infamous other woman. It had us all in splits. The next item was Pam and her group of six, who danced to a medley of Helen numbers. Pam had choreographed it well, with bold movements and gyrating hips. Soon, Mrs Sargam was beaming.

Pam's item received huge applause. Mrs Sargam praised the group and made a few suggestions about entries and exits. The dance was rehearsed one more time before Her Royal Highness was satisfied.

Eva came back on stage and announced that for the rest of the evening the band would take over.

'Eva, I want the programme to end with your song. Are you ready with it?'

'Yes, Mrs Sargam.'

Eva cleared her throat, switched the mike on and sang, '*Sare jahan se achha, Hindustan hamara, hum bulbule hain iske, yeh gulsitan hamara.*'

Eyes closed, lost in the song, her beautiful voice rang clear.

There was absolute silence, a different kind of silence. People were in awe of her. I was really beginning to like her, she was so smart, a modern woman, yet so rooted in traditions. As my admiration grew, so did Mrs Sargam's agitation.

I heard the whisper, 'Stupid woman, what is she doing,' before Mrs Sargam shouted, 'Stop this nonsense!'

Eva's eyes opened wide as if someone had slapped her.

'Mrs Chandy, we are not preparing for the annual day function in your school. The wives are hosting this party for their husbands, to entertain them. You should understand that there's a time and place for everything.'

Eva had turned pale. Eyes downcast, she stood like that for a minute. The air was charged with anticipation – we wondered how she would respond.

'What would you have me sing, Mrs Sargam?'

Mrs Sargam rolled her eyes and said, 'Something classy! You modern women should know.'

'"*Hindi hai hum, vatan hai, Hindustan hamara*", and if this isn't classy enough for an army officer and his family then I am sorry. Please find yourself some clown to do the entertaining.'

There was a long pause as everyone stared at Eva. There was respect and envy among the audience for Eva, fear too, for they knew that Eva was about to be burnt.

'You new-age wives are spoiling the image of the army! No respect for seniority!' A red-faced Mrs Sargam whispered something in Pam's ear and stomped out of the lawn with Mrs Tehlan running to catch up with her.

Later, in the jeep, Pam passed on to Eva what Mrs Sargam had said: 'I'll have her husband's head on a platter. Eva had better prepare an apology, or her husband can plan an early retirement.'

Three's a Crowd

'Of the three hundred officers currently in Jacob Hills, seven are married to women named Anita, and in the same year engraved on the pendant. Of the seven, three Anitas are residing in Jacob Hills, alive and kicking, and I have personally gone and met them. The remaining four are living in different cities or villages, and we have no means of getting any news of or to them.'

I waited for Mrs Chandy to say something. She hadn't answered my question and was instead nosing around for other details. Normally, I don't go around humouring women, but if I wanted her cooperation, I had to tell her at least a part of the information.

'Colonel, what about the initials A.R.? Surely not all the Anitas are married to men with these initials?'

'Surprisingly, none of them are married to officers with those initials. Except this one officer whose initials match. Incidentally, what do you think of Major Alex, Mrs Chandy?'

'He's a fine gentleman. Why do you ask?'

'He is Major Alex Rosario Anton.'

'His initials are A.R., but he isn't married!'

'His dossier with the Military Secretary confirms his single status. But he may have married some village belle secretly and not informed the army. There are many cases where officers have done that.'

'Major Alex doesn't seem the type to marry someone secretly.'

'Oh, one can't rule out the possibility, Mrs Chandy. I have seen very fine officers who turned out to be pigs .'

She grew silent yet again.

'Would you mind if I asked you to wear Anita's pendant on Husbands' Night? All the officers in the station will be there and maybe someone will notice it. It's worth a try.'

'I wish now she had given us his name. I wonder why she didn't when she was safe in the hospital?'

'Ma'am, that woman hadn't been safe in her own house for years. Such trauma generally leaves victims very fearful of their tormentor.'

'Somehow, I can't imagine Major Alex torturing anyone.'

'But he was at the murder scene.'

'So was I, Colonel.'

'Ma'am, I am sure you have heard that two's company and three's a crowd? What's the probability of three people turning up at an abandoned church at the same time, entirely independent of each other, and one of them being almost stabbed to death?'

George

Keep the Tail Down

'Georgy boy, have you seen how animals walk with their tails down?'

'What's your point?'

'Even animals know that they can't expose their rear and walk. Someone will come and screw them from behind. And you have one hell of a cheek prancing about with your tail up! Just apologize to the commandant's football or prepare to get royally screwed.'

'Screw you, Gary. Thanks for the advice.'

Gary meant well and I tolerated him for a while before shooing him out.

He left behind the latest edition of the *Illustrated Weekly of India* and I couldn't resist looking at the bronzed hippie on the cover, lying on her stomach on the silver sand, clad only in a bikini bottom. I flipped through the pages.

This revolutionary magazine had thrown 'respectability' right out of the window and given the pseudo-elite of the country a taste for a less prudish and more liberating lifestyle.

The editor is known to be fond of sex and scotch, and that lends great humour to its content, which ranges from anti-Sikh riots to enlightenment-eager hippies fornicating on the beaches of Goa. The English-speaking middle class, like my good friend Gary, is greatly influenced by the radical Sikh editor.

I devoted some time to a particularly disturbing article about Sikh survivors of the 1984 riots, post Indira Gandhi's assassination a year ago, and their horrific tales of torture and murder by their neighbours of many years. The article said that four days after the assassination, nearly three thousand Sikhs were massacred in systematic riots planned and led by Congress activists and sympathizers. It didn't surprise me. Nothing surprised me these days. After all, 'One man's obituary is another man's celebration.'

Brig. Sargam had called me to his office in the afternoon. His wife's blood pressure had shot up due to her confrontation with Eva. She was advised bed rest for the next few days. The brigadier demanded an apology and used a lot of fancy words. Eva had insulted his wife in front of other officers' wives and he insisted that I make her behave.

'Keep her at home if you can't handle her, Major! A wife with an attitude like that isn't going to take you far.'

Blood pounded in my head; I normally didn't give advice, but for once I felt like doing so.

'With all due respect, sir, every ruler sleeps on an anthill.

And here we are dealing with an educated woman. You can't browbeat her into an apology, especially when all she did was sing a song.'

The veins in his forehead popped. His impressive office was silent except for the loose bolt of the ceiling fan. Even the typewriters, usually clicking away in the corridor, were silent.

I was sure we had an audience on the other side of the door. The brigadier picked up the phone and asked the operator to connect him to the Military Secretary branch in Delhi that handled the careers and transfers of all officers.

I knew he was bluffing. It would take a lot more than a phone call to kick out the son of a war veteran.

He probably realized that too, for he asked the operator to connect him later. He paced across the room, his expression changing from rage to desperation.

'Major, the showdown happened in front of all the ladies residing in the station, and I stand to lose face. In my position, I can't let my wife be insulted even if there is the slightest possibility that she may be wrong. So here's the deal: your wife sings at the Husbands' Night and we forget about the whole thing.'

I was tempted to say no, but decided to pick my battles more wisely.

'I'll talk to her.'

'I am sure she can be made to see reason. Ask her to sing any goddamn song she likes, I don't care as long as she sings.'

He had waved me out of his office and later sent Gary to put some pressure on me, but I don't scare easily.

It was lunchtime. I picked up my briefcase and switched off the fan. Capt. Rana barged in just as I was leaving. He seemed angry. Well, the midterm grades were out and that could be one reason why he was here.

'You can't fail me!'

'Have I?'

'Yes … no one ever fails in this paper.'

'Apparently you did.'

He was now controlling his anger with great difficulty. I asked him to come in.

He wasn't very well turned out. He had shaved badly and there were bags under his eyes. I suspected the Old Monk was still in his system.

'Been drinking lately?'

'No, sir.'

I opened a cabinet and took out his old reports. He was indeed one of the bright stars of the course.

'Everything okay with you?'

The words had an effect I had not expected to get. The pressure that had been building for so long broke and he started to cry. God, having a grown man cry in my office was the last thing I needed. But it was my moral duty to help this idiot, and I think I knew what the problem was.

I suspected the thought of a wife and kid was too much to bear. I bet he hadn't even informed his parents about the new addition to their family.

I gave him some water and left him alone. I stepped out of the office, took out a cigarette and thought about Rana's life.

This could swing many ways – he could ruin his career, alienate his wife, become an alcoholic and eventually even commit suicide. Yes, there were cases like that, where men couldn't manage their personal lives.

Now, here's the thing: not all Casanovas are born with nerves of steel. It's so easy to sleep with a woman, like brushing your teeth or having a meal, but it's not easy to live with the same woman for the rest of your life, not unless you love her. And if you don't, married or not, you can't stay with her – a sense of responsibility is not enough to make it work. It's like smoking a cigarette – it may look good to an onlooker, but it will kill you from within.

I wanted to help him. I went back in. He had composed himself and wanted to take my leave. I asked him to sit down.

'I am fine, sir.'

'Tell me, were you just fooling around before marriage or did you have feelings for her?'

He hadn't expected this and his closed face showed that he didn't wish to discuss this issue.

'Answer me.'

'Yes, sir, I did.'

'Good, what's the problem then?'

'Having feelings is one thing, but to be forced into marriage ... that's not fair. My course mates laugh at me.'

'Oh, so you mind the arm-twisting. You hold it against her that she approached your seniors and pressured you into marrying her. Consider this: you have a respectable job, you are a man and if you sleep around, it's considered growing up. But the same rules don't apply to her. She's labelled a prostitute. Does that sound fair to you?'

He didn't meet my eyes.

'As for your fucking course mates, their brains are the size of their balls, so screw them!'

'I feel cornered, sir.'

'Stop seeing her and the baby as a responsibility! No one is punishing you. Participate a little more in your own life, stop being a selfish asshole and maybe you can turn this around.'

I didn't have anything more to say, except that I would mark his practical paper to make up for the setback in the theory paper.

'Thank you, sir! I can't believe that you'll help me in my practical.'

'We can all do with a little help, Rana. Even Heena.'

He was surprised that I knew his wife's name. Eva had told me about her.

Rana and Heena were little more than children. People think that if they can have sex and produce children, they are grown up enough to handle life. I wish that were the case.

I thought of the commandant's fat, fiftyish wife who had

thrown a plateful of food on the ground simply so she could show her power and displeasure at being served 'kacche bhature'. It was ridiculous, but there were many more like her.

I could write a book on them. I probably will when I retire from the army. Eva and I can go back to Cochin to my ancestral home, away from the madness to write poetry and make music.

The quieter life gets,
The more I am filled with music,
The noisier it gets,
The silence is deafening.
The race isn't mine,
I am born to wander ...

I take my place in a corner by the bar and eye the rest of the crowd. It's a full-moon night on a chilly October evening, and the men and women are dressed impeccably. The expensive silk and kanjeevarams are out and so are the pearls and the gold.

The lawn is lit up with decorative lights and the angithis are placed every few yards.

The waiters move among the glittering crowd with drinks and eatables on silver trays. A brass brand is playing old filmi melodies under a canopy.

The variety programme will begin as soon as the brigadier

and his wife make an entry. The time given to them is 8.30 p.m. and that's exactly when their black staff car, an ambassador, will pull into the drive. Punctuality is synonymous with the army tradition – it is one standard no officer ever fails.

For now, everyone is relaxed and having a good time.

I look around for Eva. She is easy to spot in her black maxi decorated with hand-painted white lilies. She's copied the design from a magazine on a sari that the fauji dhobi had burnt. The maxi is gathered tightly at the waist and falls to her ankles in an umbrella cut. She looks really beautiful, with little make-up and no jewellery except a small silver pendant around the neck. It's a fascinating piece with an engraved tiger on it and has the look of a family heirloom. I have never seen her wear it before. But then my wife has so many clothes and so much jewellery that it is difficult to keep up with all of it.

Standing next to me, Gary hands Col. Farhat and Col. Tehlan another drink. I have still not finished my first.

'Come on, Alex, you can have one drink with us,' Col. Tehlan prompts Alex and, despite his protests, asks the barman to pour whisky for him.

He gives the glass to Alex and says, 'A man who doesn't drink is dangerous because you don't know what goes on in his mind, but a man who drinks never lies. He's an honest man.'

It's a typical line that drinkers spit out at non-drinkers on such evenings – Col. Tehlan is your regular drinker.

After that phone call, when the colonel had asked Eva to keep her mouth shut about his daughter, he acted as if nothing had happened. I ask him how the children are doing, and his reply is, 'Ah, the usual. Climbing trees, falling down and bruising their knees.'

Eva's nurse–friend had told her that they hadn't even come around for a check-up and were probably taking Bunny to a private practitioner in Shimla.

Eva told me that Bunny hadn't come to school for the last ten days. She had been pressuring me to call upon the Tehlans, but I had a feeling we wouldn't be very welcome. Still, it was hard to believe that a six-year-old girl had been sexually abused and the father continued to drink and bullshit and the mother smiled and chatted with the other ladies.

Gary nudged me and took the empty glass from my hand. Col. Farhat and Col. Tehlan had drifted away to join some other senior officers, and Alex, Gary and I were sitting on the bar stools.

Gary whistled when Alex ordered another whisky and was mighty pleased with him.

'Alex, sher-da-puttar, now all you need is a woman and you'll be a changed man!'

The party had not even begun and the Sardar was three pegs down.

'I could do with a woman,' replied Alex.

So Alex wasn't the quiet, unassuming fellow he made himself out to be.

'Don't waste your fucking time at the bar like a loser then! We are married. We have no choice but to gaze from a distance. But, you, son-of-a-bitch, just walk up to any woman and ask her.'

Gary got off his stool and pushed him in the direction of the women standing close to the bar.

'Which one?' asked Alex, a little bemused.

Gary looked around and said, 'That one! I bet you a hundred, she'll be quite willing.'

He pointed out a smartly dressed woman with slightly oriental features in a Baku, the traditional Sikkimese dress. She was speaking to a couple and holding a glass of what seems like rum in her hand.

'You know her?' Alex asked Gary.

'No, Alex, I don't and you don't need to know her either to sleep with her.'

My patience with this exchange was wearing thin. 'Gary, how can you pick a random woman and say that she'll be willing?'

Gary lifted his glass and said in a Punjabi accent, 'Peeti hai, toh deti hai, dost!' If she drinks, she's willing to give it away.

Despite the crudity of the remark, we all laughed. I looked for Pam and saw her sitting on a sofa, chatting with the ladies and sipping her wine. I guess Gary was right then.

I noticed Rana's wife, Heena. She was sitting in a corner

alone, waiting, wondering if someone would occupy the chair next to her. Eventually someone would, but that wouldn't lessen her sense of alienation.

Her husband was at the other bar, and like everyone else, was dressed in a three-piece suit. A cigarette between his lips and a glass in one hand, he was chatting away with his course mates. It was difficult to believe that this man had been sobbing in my office just the day before. He was calm and debonair now. Oh, well, like the old joke goes, a man has got to be in the army if he's stressed, depressed and still well dressed. I saw no hope for him.

Suddenly, the band picked up and that meant the guest of honour had arrived. Col. Tehlan and Col. Farhat, followed by their wives, stood at attention, carrying bouquets, at the entrance of the lawn.

The commandant and his wife got out of the car, and a young lieutenant held the door open for them. They walked in like royalty and were greeted sycophantically by the officers and their wives.

Once they settled down on the sofa, the lights were dimmed. The MC appeared on stage and started to sing praises of Mrs Sargam: her work in organizing the welfare programme for the jawans' wives and how it had inspired all the ladies. Bullshit!

The programme finally commenced with a skit about two women, the wife and the other woman, fighting over a man. It went on for about twenty minutes and was hilarious enough to elicit a few genuine laughs.

Next was a dance performance by six women, led by Pam, dressed in red-and-gold harem pants and tight-fitting, shimmering blouses that reached their navels.

They had set their hair in the popular style of the time, a bob. Pam took centre stage and moved her belly to the music of Helen's classic, '*Piya tu ab toh aja*'.

The movements were well coordinated, bold but not brazen. The hooting and whistling continued throughout the performance, and the sexy hip gyrations left the officers panting for more.

I could see Brig. Sargam and his wife applauding loudly, and words like 'bravo', 'well done' and 'good show' were thrown at the dancers. Amidst much applause and cat calls, Pam and her gang bowed and retreated from the stage.

I clapped too, but my heart was beating faster, not because of the dance but because Eva was to go on next. For a minute I was tempted to ask her to call it off. I didn't want her to get hurt.

I debated about stopping her from making a fool of herself, but a little voice in my head said, 'You love her and you have got to stand by her even if she chose to recite, "Twinkle twinkle little star".'

I watched her walk slowly towards the mike and receive a lukewarm welcome. The lights went out and the spotlight was on her. Eva looked rather dainty on that big stage. The light beam caught the silver around her neck, which gleamed, as did the big white lilies on her dress.

Her clear voice was accompanied by the flute and created a harmony that succeeded in wiping the smirks and the disbelief off the audience's faces within the first few notes. There were no cat calls, just silence.

'*Hindi hai hum, vatan hai, Hindustan hamara.*' As the momentum built, many officers joined in. The new voices lent power to the spirit of the song and carried it deep into our hearts.

Patriotism is at the very core of a soldier's being. He may or may not be ready, but a soldier willingly puts his life on the line to protect his countrymen. When his time comes, there is no fear of death, just the steely resolve that the enemy must not succeed.

I had seen this spirit many times in the eyes of the men, oftentimes fighting enemies more powerful than them. Yes, this love for the country had brought all of us where we were today. I had lost sight of my reasons for a while, but seeing Eva's steadfastness and the fierce sentiments of my fellow officers, I felt that old spirit rise again, if only for a while.

Once the song ended, the men gave her a standing ovation, even as the ladies stayed stuck to their chairs. I hugged her once she got off the stage.

Volleys of compliments were being thrown her way and even the brigadier congratulated her, but his wife stayed put; her face an expressionless mask.

The band began to play and I steered Eva onto the dance floor. I could feel her relaxing in my arms.

'So?' she asked.

'You outshone the moon tonight.'

'Really, was I good?'

'Beautiful. For a minute there, I had butterflies in my stomach.'

She smiled and I wanted to crush her in my arms. We danced on for two more numbers. We got off the floor to have a drink and bumped straight into Pam. She had changed into a silk sari, but kept her bob cut wig on. She resembled those svelte vamps in the movies who pout and bat their eyelids coyly.

We congratulated her on her performance, but she brushed it aside, saying Eva was the real show stealer.

Her glass was empty and I offered to refill it.

There was a big rush at the bar. While I waited my turn, I saw Maj. Vikram gulp down his drink and stare at a painfully thin woman speaking animatedly to an officer. There was a strange expression on Vikram's face, a kind of powerless rage. It deepened when the woman raised her glass in his direction and left with the other man. He was holding his glass so tightly that I thought it would break.

I returned in about ten minutes to the spot where I had left Pam and Eva, but they were nowhere to be seen.

I looked around. The dance floor was packed and there wasn't an inch of space to move around. In the dim light I was unsure if Eva and Pam were on the floor. It was a possibility. The moment the YOs saw ladies unattended, they flocked to ask them for a dance.

For a minute, I thought I should find her; sometimes an officer or two could get too drunk and act rowdy. But it was just ten and the waiters were serving a rich cream almond soup. Nothing bad usually happened before dinner.

I sat down to enjoy my soup and fine-tune a little something that had popped up in my head while Eva was singing on the stage, frail yet fearless.

There's something moving about courage,
The innocence behind daring,
You may label it foolhardy,
But that will only bring on a smile,
That's strength right there, raw, vulnerable,
To do many a difficult thing,
The right ones, if she can.

On the Dance Floor

I didn't know who we were dancing with, but Pam seemed to know all the youngsters. Most of them knew only one dance step and a rather odd one. They would snap their fingers and keep shifting their weight from one foot to the other.

A few flamboyant ones knew a mix of foxtrot and jazz and set the floor on fire. Soon the beat changed and it was time for a slow dance. More couples joined in, adding to the rush. It was becoming difficult to breathe. I had to get out.

I didn't say bye to Pam, or she would have tried to stop me. I elbowed my way off the floor. I had almost left, when someone pulled me back, grabbing the chain around my neck. I felt such excruciating pain around my neck that tears swam into my eyes. The pressure kept building. I couldn't understand what was happening. Was someone trying to choke me?

There was someone behind me, pressing me against his body. He had to be a tall man to shield me from the crowd around us. My hands went to my throat again and I realized that the pendant was no longer around my neck.

I wanted to scream for help. I could see George sitting at a distance, but no sound would leave my lips. I tried to attract the attention of people around me, but everyone was so absorbed in their partners that no one spared me a glance.

In sheer panic, I dug my heel into my captor's left foot. He cried out and let me go. I rubbed my neck. I wanted to turn and see who was behind me, but I was scared. In the split second that I took to decide what to do, someone threw a protective arm around me.

Maj. Alex was looking at me with concern in his eyes. He had looked at the lady in the church with that same expression – and she had died.

'I'll escort you off the floor, Ma'am.'

'No!'

I started pushing my way out and he was right behind me. Col. Sampat was right about Alex. He must have wanted the pendant badly; why else would he attack me in public?

George saw me staggering towards him and lines of worry formed on his forehead, deepening when he came close.

'Eva, what happened to your neck? There's a red line running across it.'

He ran his fingers across and it hurt. I saw Alex coming towards us and urged George to take me home.

'Without dinner? What's wrong?'

I didn't know what to say, Alex was barely four feet away.

I caught hold of George's hand and dragged him to the parking lot. George looked back and saw Alex following us. I snapped at him to hurry up.

George signalled the driver and we got into the jeep.

The moment we reached home, I rushed to examine my neck in the mirror.

It wasn't really that bad; just a faint red line and a stinging sensation. I relaxed a little. It was my fear that had made me react this way. I drank some water while George waited for me to say something.

I didn't feel so upset now and decided against telling him anything. He would get angry. It was a foolish thing to do – wear a dead woman's jewellery to get her killer to react. Well, we got a reaction and I wonder what Col. Sampat would do next. He had said he'd be at the party, but I hadn't seen him.

I still had to deal with George. I tried to kiss him, but he warded me off. Instead, he held my hand and looked at my face. He was worried earlier; now he seemed almost angry.

'Did someone misbehave with you?'

And just like that, I told George everything – from Wilhelmina giving me the pendant to Col. Sampat approaching me to wear it to the party.

'Stupid woman! Why didn't you tell me any of this before?'

'Precisely because I didn't want to be called stupid!'

He started pacing the room.

'Eva, it still can't be Alex. You need to be made of sterner stuff to commit murder.'

'George, you're saying this? You were the one who was most suspicious of him! Besides, I am telling you, he was right behind me.'

'You saw him?'

'Yes. When I turned around, he was there.'

'Eva, if Alex was the murderer, the woman in the hospital would have told you or someone about him. And why would he carry her to the hospital?'

'She was scared stiff, George, you should have seen her! And if he didn't have anything to do with the dead woman, what did he need the pendant for?'

'I am meeting the colonel tomorrow and asking that crazy bastard why he's got you involved in all this!'

I remembered Col. Sampat's parting words, 'In my village, they believe that one should not touch, let alone wear, the jewellery of a married woman who has suffered a violent death – not if she was wearing that object when she died. Her sorrows and desires tend to linger on in her favourite things. I hope you don't believe in all this superstitious nonsense?.'

Bunny

At Home

Mummy is very angry that I got hurt. She doesn't send me to school and treats me very badly till papa comes from office and asks for me. I want to go to school and play with my friends, but she doesn't let me.

Yesterday, she shouted at Papa and he slapped her. Then she said, 'I'll take the children and go away.'

I don't want to go with Mummy. I want to stay with Papa. Only Sunny likes her. Even Papa doesn't like her.

She sleeps in our room with Mini and me. Mini is very happy that Mummy sleeps with us, but I don't like it.

Now Papa doesn't come to tell me my bedtime story.

I hate Mummy. She's always shouting at us.

The doctor says that I should tell Mummy if someone tries to touch me there. They'll catch the bad man and send him to jail. I look at Mummy, she's looking at me. I look at Papa and he's smiling at me.

We come back home from the party and, on the way, Papa buys me two ice creams.

The doctor said, 'You are a brave girl, Bunny, and if someone misbehaves with you, you must tell your Mummy.'

Tell Mummy? Doesn't Mummy know? I think she does.

Saryu

The Key Club

There was a big glass bowl on the centre table. As Vikram and I entered the Sinhas' living room, he dropped the car keys into the bowl. There were already three elaborate key chains in there before ours. I knew the other couples – what I did not know was that they too were a part of the club. It came as a shock that the pretty, convent-educated wives, who came from big cities, women who were not in the least me, chose to be here. Their husbands too, unlike Vikram, were polished and sophisticated. Everyone mingled easily.

I was in a daze. Had I not dreamt of being better educated or being born in a high-class family? These men and women seemed to posses all the attributes I had longed for: looks, carriage and lineage, and yet they were no better than Vikram and I. At least we had our complexes to blame for our actions, but what about these picture-perfect couples?

I felt very unsure of myself. Men I could handle, but the

women had me tongue-tied. I was no match for their superior class and elegance.

There were four couples besides us and one forced bachelor. The men smoked in the balcony, while the women laid the chicken and mutton kebabs on the counter. There were all kinds of bottles on the table: wine, whisky, rum, scotch and beer. A silver icebox was filled with ice and, going by the empty soda bottles, the men and women were well on their way to getting drunk.

I greeted the hostess. She asked me what I would like to drink.

I refused the drink and asked for water. Pam came out of the kitchen laughing, saying, 'Have a drink, Saryu. It'll help you loosen up.'

I took the drink and put it on the side table. Life had made me 'loose' enough, I didn't need a drink to shed my inhibitions. I just wanted to observe these high-class people in their own milieu. They drank too much, laughed too much and sized each other up as prospective sleeping partners.

Not everyone was like that, but the successful ones more often than not fell into one trap or the other. My father would say that if a man had money and power, sex was bound to follow. I wasn't sure what drove these people to such a lifestyle. I was curious.

Pam came and sat next to me on the sofa. Her face was flushed and the glass was tilting dangerously in her hand. I had to ask her before I lost the nerve.

'Why do you come here, Pam?'

'To have fun.'

'You don't get enough fun at home?' It slipped out.

She pulled me close and whispered in my ear, 'I don't like Gary's long hair, it smells. And some of these young buggers have more staying power. You know what I mean.'

Pam, despite being dangerously seductive, is a funny woman.

'Doesn't Gary mind?'

'Look, honey, after a point, you are very comfy with each other, but also bored to death, much like a cow tethered to a post. A little grazing on the side keeps the cow healthy and satisfied.'

I have found that going down on a man is far easier than sucking up to a woman and, frankly, lately I don't feel like sucking up to anyone.

'I think it's a like a disease, like an itchy rash that spreads all over.'

'Well, hello, you are one to talk, Miss Big Mouth.' Pam guffawed.

The pot-bellied colonel had spread nasty rumours about me before he left for his new post. He ensured that it would counter anything I might have to say about him and his aborted child.

'Pam, if I had your brains and education, I wouldn't be hopping in and out of beds.'

'Don't be all high and mighty, Saryu, and use your inferior

background as an excuse. You think education can fix the itch down there? Then go get a degree, who's to stop you? Your husband?'

We both looked in Vikram's direction. He cut a drab figure, a wannabe like me, who wanted attention and hoped to get somewhere in life.

Vikram, I realized, was a wimp.

Pam had given me something to think about, but it would have to wait. The party was just warming up and the men returned to the living room. Someone switched on the the record player and jazz played in the background. The noise went up a notch and the alcohol kept flowing till it was difficult to make out what was being said.

Gary was the most vocal and kept everyone entertained. It seemed like a regular get together, with food, drinks and conversation.

When the clock struck twelve, the innocent party turned into something else altogether. The host picked up the bowl with the car keys and showed it around to the men. One by one, each man picked up a car key and held it up for the women to see. The women recognized their keys and went with the man who held it up.

Gary was holding our car keys. I looked at Vikram, he looked away. Apparently, he was spending the night right here with our hostess, the nicely plump Mrs Sinha. I had no choice but to lug Gary home for the night; Pam had already left with the forced bachelor.

Gary was charming as ever and kept the conversation going. On my part, I could only think of what Pam had said about his hair.

I fumbled through my bag for the house keys and opened the front door. We walked in. I was becoming increasingly nervous. I asked if he would like a drink. He didn't need one, but I did and he agreed. As I took out the glasses from the bar, I could feel the heat of his gaze. I poured a large in his glass and then some more. I didn't bother with adding water. He took a sip and instantly closed his eyes as the whisky stung his throat.

'That's a strong drink! Are you trying to put me to sleep?'

I smiled and sat opposite him on the sofa.

'I thought it would be a good idea to find out what makes you tick,' I said, trying my best to hide my anxiety.

'Beautiful women like you.'

Gary knew how to lie.

'Your wife's beautiful. Why do you drag her into this?'

He started to laugh and paused to say, 'Darling, it's my wife who's oversexed. I am perfectly happy with the way things are, but she wants to experiment. I am simply obliging her.'

'And you let her? That can't be true. You are a man and she's a woman ...' I was baffled.

'Saryu, I don't know if you would understand, but deep down men and women are not very different. Some have a greater appetite for sex and they don't turn away from it.

Most people who conform to social norms, secretly long to fly. Everyone, in the confines of his or her mind, is a highly sexual creature. If you could peep into other people's heads, you would see that there are far more perverted people than us. Did you hear what happened with the poor Tehlans? Never mind.'

He finished his drink in one gulp, shook his head hard once and lunged at me saying, 'Sex is the most basic biological urge. How does one repress it, Saryu?'

His arms locked around me and his body blocked my exit. I had a choice; I could fly with him for a while or chase a long cherished dream of becoming my own woman.

I asked him to give me a minute to change. He was about to refuse, when I pulled him close and said, 'It'll be worth the wait.' Grinning, he made way. I walked to the room and slammed the door shut.

Some time passed. He knocked many times, but I didn't open the door.

'It's your loss, lady.'

Finally he gave up. Vikram found him fast asleep on the living room floor when he returned at six in the morning after what I assumed was a long and rewarding night.

Col. Sampat

The List

We were walking around the huge campus of Jacob Hills, having gotten past the initial hiccup of Maj. Chandy being furious about his wife's involvement in the inquiry of the dead woman's murder.

I was scheduled to attend the Husbands' Night party, but a street fight between civilians and army personnel had erupted on Mall Road, and I had to be present there to liaise with the local authorities.

Maj. Chandy was not convinced about Maj. Alex's involvement in the incident that took place that night, but his wife was adamant that it was he who had attacked her.

Before coming to meet Maj. Chandy, I had walked over to the classroom where Maj. Alex was giving a lecture. I was impressed by how enthusiastically he taught the youngsters. It made me wonder if a man so passionate about his profession, and the values of integrity and uprightness associated with it, could torture a woman to death.

And even if he was our guy, where would he have kept Anita while she was alive? As a bachelor, he was allotted a bachelor's room in the east wing of Jacob Hall with the other instructors. A woman couldn't stay there, let alone slip in or out unnoticed.

It was a long shot and nothing seemed to fall in place as far as he was concerned. I was beginning to believe that it was fate indeed that had brought Anita, Mrs Chandy and Maj. Alex to the church that day.

Furthermore, Alex's take on the Husbands' Night incident was different from Mrs Chandy's.

'She was definitely a little tipsy. I tried to help her off the dance floor, but she seemed agitated and just took off.'

'What did you think of the silver pendant?'

'What pendant?'

He had asked the question with such transparent honesty that I was quite sure he didn't know anything about the pendant.

'Drunk or not, Mrs Chandy is adamant that it was you who attacked her, and she doesn't seem like the sort of woman who'd scream wolf for no reason. So, you tell me, Major, what is it that you have been hiding from me?'

'Every man is entitled to a few secrets, Colonel, but honest to God, I didn't take the pendant. I remember Mrs Chandy was on the stage that night and created quite a furore with her song. Your man could have seen the pendant around her neck and come to claim it.'

He had made a good point; Mrs Chandy was definitely eye candy.

The only way forward now was to track down the other four officers in Jacob Hills who were married to women named Anita. I had so far managed to get some cursory information on them – none of which seemed promising.

Maj. Chandy requested me to share the list of officers with him. Being an instructor at the War College, it would be easier for him to access information about them. I gave him the list without hesitation. His father still had a pull in high places; doors would open far more easily for him.

He studied the list for a moment and said, 'I know two of these officers; they play squash at the Tiller's Club. I can catch them there.'

'You'll have to be careful, Major Chandy. The murderer knows your wife. From here on, let's assume that he knows more about us than we do about him. Don't take any unnecessary risks. We don't know what we are dealing with here.'

'Don't worry, Colonel, I'll take care. I'll also get in touch with the other two officers. Since they are here without their wives, the bar at the club will be a good place to find them.'

'I appreciate your help, Major. There's one more thing ... do you think Mrs Chandy could persuade her student Junaira to give her a description of the man who burnt her?'

Garba Papa

It was the last period of the day and the children were drawing. I wanted to go and see what Junaira had drawn, but didn't wish to alarm her, so I waited for everyone to come and deposit their sheets on my desk.

Bunny had returned to class and was aggressively rubbing a crayon on her sheet.

Once they had finished drawing, I walked nonchalantly to my chair, quickly leafed through and located the sheet with Junaira's name at the bottom.

I was disappointed. She had drawn a big circle, more like an amoeba with eyes, and had filled it with a yellow crayon.

So much for instructing the children to draw something or someone they feared or didn't like. It would help them get rid of their fear.

I put her sheet aside and looked at the others. Some had drawn animals, like a dog or a lion, and the others had drawn monster shapes. Only Bunny had drawn a face, a rather sinister one – a square with big eyes and a crooked nose drawn with a black crayon. She had coloured the lips red and put a big bindi between the eyes.

I was startled to say the least. She had drawn a picture of her mother. Why did Bunny fear her mother?

I put the sketch aside and hoped to speak to Bunny after class. She seemed subdued, not her usual, chirpy self. Her older brother Sunny had come to drop her to school and she was to go home with him. The batman had been changed.

It's tough being a child in an adult's world, every day their innocence dies a little. Slowly they learn to screen their emotions, lie, hide and pretend to be strong, like us. Isn't that how we grown-ups live, pretending to be strong?

At Col. Sampat's insistence, I tried to speak to Junaira about her burn mark, but she stared at me blankly.

'Junaira, what is the yellow circle you have drawn?'

'Garba papa.'

'The cartoon on TV?'

'No, that's Bunny's papa.'

'Are you scared of Bunny's papa?'

'He's not nice.'

Junaira ran away, leaving me to make sense of Garba papa and why she didn't like Bunny's father. The cartoon was shown every Sunday morning on Doordarshan and all the children were crazy about it. Garba papa was a lovable figure, a yellow bouncing blob with kind eyes and two dots in place of a nose.

Could she be saying that Bunny's father was as huge as Garba papa?

On the other hand was Bunny's hatred for her mother. There was too much happening in a first grade schoolteacher's life. More would follow once George met the officers on the list.

George being George had been overprotective to the point of being overbearing lately. He had even forbidden me from going for my evening walks. I paid no attention and decided to walk back home after the evening annual day function rehearsal.

It was a quarter to five and the sun was mellowing. I felt like jogging and slung my bag on my shoulder and began a slow jog downhill. The grey track pants were a size big, but the pink jacket was a good fit.

I did a kilometre without losing breath, but the uphill climb had me panting within minutes. What is a workout without a little sweat? I persisted, though I had slowed down to an ant's pace.

The breeze would kiss the sweat away and coax me into running a little further. A lot of officers who were out for their evening games greeted me on the way. I reached a hillock, slowed down and then completely stopped to catch my breath. The sunset looked breathtaking, the last rays of the orange sun hanging just above the mountains and then starting to dip rapidly.

'Good evening, Ma'am.'

Maj. Alex had crept up on me again. In my twenty-four years of life, I had striven to never be rude to anyone but this one time would be an exception.

'I just wished to clear the air,' he said, sweat dripping down his face. Could he have been following me?

'Major Alex, I don't wish to discuss anything with you. Please speak to my husband if you have to.' I started to jog away from him, but he followed and ran by my side.

We jogged silently. I was uncomfortably aware of him. What if he pushed me down the hill? They wouldn't find my body for a long time.

'Look ...'

I ignored him. But he persisted and spoke of Col. Sampat's visit.

'He was asking about some pendant that you were wearing at the party. Did you lose it?'

I was starting to get really angry. He knew very well that I had lost it – he had snatched it from around my neck!

'Get away from me, or I'll scream for help!' I couldn't take it any more.

He stopped abruptly and said, 'I am sorry for intruding, Ma'am. Enjoy your run.'

Now it was my turn to feel bad. I had not expected him to just apologize and leave me alone. I stared after him.

I remembered him anxiously praying for Anita at the hospital.

I felt unsure. Had paranoia coloured my vision? There were a lot of officers on the dance floor that day, could I have been wrong?

The year engraved on the pendant was 1982, which meant that Anita must have been at least twenty-one at the time of her marriage.

Some of the wives I knew had gotten married as young as nineteen. Parents were always in such a hurry to settle their daughters down before they ran away or embarrassed them over some good-for-nothing boy.

I had been lucky to have parents who were more interested in giving me an education than in marrying me off.

In the seventies, families were very strict about caste and religion. An inter-caste marriage meant that the parents considered their daughter dead and cut her out of their lives and hearts.

Maybe that was the reason no one came looking for Anita.

I studied the list while George took a shower. He had written something in pencil in front of each name.

Maj. Bedi - six-month course, wife living with in-laws in Ludhiana, two sons, smokes

Maj. Chattopadhyay - instructor in the Tactical Wing, wife is an airhostess, Delhi, no children, smokes occasionally

Maj. Thakur - in three-month course, wife staying in Separated Family (SF) accommodation, Kanpur, no children, smokes

Lt. Col. Sharma - in three-month course, wife and two daughters, Jammu, doesn't smoke

They all seemed like regular people with regular lives. None of them sounded like a killer. Only the Bengali surname 'Chattopadhyay' seemed a little promising.

But I had a feeling it wasn't going to be that easy. It would take more than a surname to find a man who had killed his wife in cold blood.

Both Maj. Chattopadhyay and Maj. Thakur seemed to fit the husband's profile because they didn't have children which is what Anita had mentioned to me that day in the hospital. Plus, both of them smoked which explained the burn marks.

George had said that finding the killer wasn't going to be easy but, in his words, 'elimination on the basis of verification' would simplify the process for us. He was using his resources and his father's to track down the wives of these men. I was surprised at how sincerely he had taken it up. He must have been really bored teaching at the college.

I took a pencil from the pen stand on George's study table and wrote another name on the paper.

Maj. Alex Rosario Anton???

There was something about him that didn't seem right and until I knew what it was, I wasn't going to rest. This would require a little skill on my part, but I was sure that George would eventually see my point.

I heard the bathroom door open and George called out to me for a towel. I thought I had put a towel in there but maybe I had forgotten to hang it. He called out again and I hurried towards the bathroom with the towel in my hand, lest he came out just like that, dripping water all over the floor.

He looked cute, peeping through the door, water trickling down his hair. I threw the towel at his face, and he pulled me in.

'George, I'll get wet, let go of me!'

He smiled and pushed me under the shower.

'I swear, I could kill you. Look what you've done to my clothes!'

'Eva, live a little!'

I lunged at him and he caught me in his arms. The contact with his wet, naked body sent an electric current coursing through me. I recoiled and then gave in.

He took my mouth in his, rivulets of water ran down our faces and then it didn't matter where I was.

He lifted the dress off me effortlessly – he had had a lot of practice at that. I threw water in his eyes and locked his lips with mine.

An unhurried, deliberately slow duel of wills followed

under the waterfall as the water cleansed our hearts and minds.

There was something so purifying about being in water. I remember playing in the tub for hours as a child, inventing little games with water. Now the game had changed, but at heart, we were still children, playing with life, with each other. We splashed water and soaped each other until bubbles floated in the air and misted the windowpanes and the mirror. There was such happiness in George's eyes, I felt that this was how we were meant to live in His creation, stop the pretence and be playful. I wiped the mirror with the towel, and he immediately lifted me up and held me against the opposite wall. In the mirror, I saw his broad back and narrow hips covering my body. I wasn't sure if his leg was ready for that kind of strain, but it must have been, for I felt a sudden heat inside of me. The water pouring on our heads added to the frenzy of him pounding away.

But these games, this playfulness is not for everybody. Two images flashed in my mind as I looked in the mirror – the burn marks on Anita's navel and the blood trickling down Bunny's tender thighs.

Heena

The Fall

I was more terrified than I had ever been before. The doctor had said I might lose the baby. My haemoglobin count was very low.

'Normally women with a low haemoglobin count are unable to conceive, and if they do, they usually have a miscarriage in their first trimester,' she had said.

She sent me home with medicines and a lot of advice, and the instruction that I was to bring my husband along for next week's check-up. I wasn't going to mention a word to Rana. He would be happy if I lost the baby.

He had become very quiet lately. He didn't go out as much, but that was because his exams were to start soon. He behaved cordially with me and ate whatever I put on the table. Like a paying guest, he left in the morning, came home in the evening, finished his studies and went to sleep, bidding me a casual goodnight.

Many times during the night, I wanted to wake him up

and talk to him. I had nothing important to say – I just wanted to talk of mundane matters, to drive the loneliness away.

There was a time when my eyes would close even before my head hit the pillow, but I hadn't had a sound night's sleep since I married Rana. So, now, apart from low haemoglobin and high blood pressure, I suffered from insomnia. No one cared what was happening to me.

Ammi did, but she had her own life now; she was soon to be married to Imran chacha, and I didn't want to burden her any more with the choices I had made. She was finally going to be able to steal a little happiness from the life that was fast running out of her.

I thought of Abba. Had he been alive, my circumstances would have been different. Would he have protected me? Abba's frail body at the time of his death popped up in my head. He too had died a broken man, disillusioned with fate. It's a good thing he wasn't around to see the shame I had brought upon the family.

No, there is no protection for the fallen. They keep falling deeper and deeper.

My mind was my own enemy now, it tortured me day and night with strange thoughts. I wanted to die but I also wanted to live, and while I lived, I wanted to be truly loved. I couldn't seem to do either: live or die.

I slipped out of bed gently so as not to disturb Rana, and went out into the small lawn. There was a waning moon in the sky. I urged her to not let the madness take hold of me, to protect my child from my insane thoughts.

The baby and I walked on the grass. It was chilly, but I didn't feel like going back inside. I stayed inside the whole day, stitching black flower-shaped patches on red cushions for the living room, or crocheting outfits for the little one, but time passed slowly when there was no one to talk to.

I could always speak to the trees, the stars and the moon. They listened and gave me the answers I wanted to hear. In my saner moments I laughed at myself, 'Look, no one is there to hear poor Heena, so she speaks to the sky.'

My conversation was interrupted by a sudden movement in a nearby bush. Thinking it to be some wild animal from the jungle, I hurried indoors. There was dew on the grass and suddenly, I felt my feet slipping.

I fell flat on my back. The pain was indescribable. I yelled loudly and clutched my stomach.

'God, please! Don't take my baby away from me!' I kept screaming as the tears started to flow. Rana came out, quickly picked me up and took me inside. He asked me to stop crying and lie still, but the pain was unbearable. I moved a lot.

I lifted my head to see where he was, but he had left me again. Just like that.

A few minutes later, he came back into the room with the neighbours, picked me up again, put me in the back seat of a Fiat and held me close.

We reached the hospital and I was admitted. A nurse examined me and then a doctor. I asked them if the baby was all right, but they didn't answer and asked me to calm down.

I saw Rana leaning against a wall in the room, looking at the mosaic floor. He looked up and saw me staring at him. Some impulse made me mouth 'I love you' to him.

He turned abruptly and left. I hated myself.

I closed my eyes, hoping that I would never have to open them again.

I woke up in the morning to the sound of silence. No one was holding my hand or sitting on a chair waiting for me to wake up. I wanted to laugh at the cruelty of it all.

The nurse came in and said that I was fine, and that nothing had happened to the baby. But my blood pressure had shot up in the night. She advised me not to get agitated – it could harm the baby.

'I'll send your husband in.'

'He's here?'

'Of course, he's here.'

That must seem like a strange question coming from a pregnant wife.

Rana came in and stood at the foot of the bed, his head hanging.

'The doctor says the baby is fine.'

He didn't care about the baby or me. I just wanted him to leave. I had nothing to say, so I didn't and just looked away.

'You know last night, when you said to me ...'

'Go away!' I shouted at him.

He didn't leave, just turned his face away. Then he came and took my hand. I tried to snatch it away, but he wouldn't let go. I looked up to find him weeping.

I didn't understand why he was crying.

'I am sorry. I left the room last night because I didn't want to cry in front of so many people.' And just like that, both of us started to weep. There was so much unsaid.

Even through my tears, I was beginning to see that if we didn't give up on those we loved, they would come around.

George

Anita's A.R.

The telephone had been ringing the whole morning, bringing news of all kinds. The officers on the list who had no children were the first on my radar. A mother can never leave her children behind, and even if she did, the father wouldn't know what to do with them. Anita had told Eva that she had no children.

Both Maj. Thakur and Maj. Chattopadhyay were childless. My old unit was posted in Kanpur and I had requested a chap to be sent over to the SF quarters to discreetly verify if a Mrs Thakur lived there.

She did, the neighbours confirmed it. But she had taken off to stay with her parents for two months after her husband left for the course. Nobody knew which part of the country she had gone to.

It was perfectly normal for wives to lock up the house and go to their parents in the absence of their husbands. But we couldn't be sure if she was actually at her parents'. That put Maj. Thakur in the red.

I put a cross against Maj. Chattopadhyay. Papa had tracked the major's wife to an Indian Airlines' office, and had even gone and met her on some pretext. Trust Papa to be game for chatting up pretty, young things.

The major's chatty wife had told Papa that she was coming to Jacob Hall next month to visit her instructor husband. That let Maj. Chattopadhyay off the hook.

Maj. Bedi's family was fairly easy to track. Papa had asked a YO from the unit posted nearest to Ludhiana to pay his wife a visit. He reported back that the major's twins were a nightmare and the young mother had spoilt them silly.

The next name on the list was Lt. Col. Sharma's. Though I had not been able to track his family in Jammu, I was confident that a man who had the responsibility of two daughters on his head needed his wife around.

The last name was in Eva's handwriting. I had asked Papa to find out something about him, but the only thing he could come up with was the story behind Maj. Alex's award – the dim-wittedness that had led his men to death.

Eva was convinced there was something fishy going on with Alex; she called it her woman's intuition. I would call it nonsense, but not to her face.

I adored this about her. The confidence with which she made all those sweeping statements about this or that, and said, 'George, my sixth sense is very strong.'

Strong often turned out to be wrong, but I rarely pointed

that out to her. That was the key to our happy marriage – listen carefully to everything she says, just don't act on it.

The phone rang, it was Pam. I coochie-cooed into the receiver, enough to get her to help me with my problem. I promised to see her in the evening and went back to my detective work.

I circled Maj. Thakur's name.

The phone rang again and Col. Tehlan's PA informed me that 'sahib' would like to see me immediately. I dreaded meeting that man; things had become really awkward in the last few days.

Regular updates from Eva told me that he and his wife had been doing little to help Bunny.

I walked up to his office and told the PA to inform Col. Tehlan. The PA was a wiry, funny looking fellow who knocked a couple of files in his haste to uncross his legs and stand up to salute me.

'Jai Hind, sahib. Colonel sahib is waiting for you.'

I thanked Akal Singh and went into the colonel's office.

Col. Tehlan did not offer me a seat, so I stood at attention. He was signing some documents and kept me waiting till he was done. He took off his glasses and addressed me, 'Chandy, I don't care if you are the blue-eyed boy of the commandant or your father is a three-star general, you educate your wife and tell her to mind her own bloody business.'

Oh, no, what had Eva done this time?

'Your wife wrote a little note on my daughter's drawing book, and asked her to show it to my wife. It really upset her.'

'Sir.' I really did not want to know what was in the note.

'Ask your wife to check with you before writing such notes.' He put his glasses on again and read from a sheet of paper, "The sketch shows child's fear of an authority figure and shows the need of careful handling and affection.'

He threw the sketch at me. I picked it up and looked at the drawing. Bunny's drawing skills were nothing to talk about, but the image on the paper reminded me of Mrs Tehlan. The child had drawn the face and then doodled over it with a black crayon.

I had to agree with Eva. Bunny seemed to be petrified of her mother.

He had still not asked me to sit; it appeared we were headed for a showdown. I was beginning to realize that my career, apart from my own shortcomings, was going to be greatly shortened by my wife's active interest in the welfare of others.

It was a funny thought and I had to struggle to suppress a smile. Then I made rather lame attempts to appease my boss. But how was I to do that without bringing up the sensitive topic of Bunny's abuse?

At Eva's behest, I had written to an old psychiatrist friend, Rajan, and he had called up two nights ago from London to find out more about the child.

Eva's concern was simple: if the hospital examination confirmed that there was penetration and the child was being sexually abused, why had she not mentioned it to anyone? Eva's concerted attempt at questioning Bunny about it had met with a blank face. The child had appeared not to understand anything, and the only time she had showed a violent reaction was when Eva had brought up her mother.

After listening to Eva's questions, Rajan suggested the cause could be 'disassociation', which was fairly common in children who had suffered repeated physical, sexual, and/ or emotional abuse. He explained disassociation to be a normal process that all of us experience while watching a movie, reading a good book or simply day dreaming, whereby we lose touch with the immediate surroundings for a while.

'In the case of abuse, the child just disassociates himself or herself from the ongoing abuse to cope with the trauma of the experience. In short, they block the events out and have no memory of it.'

That appeared to be a probable reason for Bunny's behaviour. She seemed so unaffected by the whole thing.

Rajan advised that the child needed medical help and counselling, but before that we needed to ensure that the child was not still being abused or threatened.

We told him that the best we could do was raise the issue with her parents. Rajan's reply had taken the wind out our sails.

'What if the mother is abusing the child, George?'

Eva had jumped to Mrs Tehlan's defence, saying that no matter how lousy a mother she may be, she couldn't have abused Bunny.

'In seventy per cent of child abuse cases in the UK, the father, mother, uncle or brother is involved. You must have a word with the parents.'

The suggestion of speaking to my boss at that point had seemed ludicrous. We had made our peace with the situation, thinking that surely the parents would know how to handle their child better.

But seeing Tehlan now, being so unreasonable about the sketch, when even I could tell that the child was asking for help, I was very troubled.

Well, to hell with him. A young life is more important than this man's or his wife's foolish pride.

'Sir, what my wife is trying to say here is that the child is scared and who wouldn't be after such a traumatic experience? It's the child's way of asking for help and we should ...'

'Major Chandy, I didn't call you to ask your opinion, so shut the fuck up and listen. You are up for a warning letter for not adhering to the code of conduct ... and don't think it's a small matter or that I'll let you get away with it.'

He went on for about five minutes, at the end of which he threw me out of his office. I was almost out, when something made me turn and say, 'I am all right with whatever letters you plan to send me, but you ought to take better care of your child. If you can't, then maybe you should report it to the police. Child abuse isn't a small matter either.'

I stayed long enough to see his face go white and hands ball into tight fists. He seemed angry, but if my ten years in the army had taught me anything, it was to recognize when a man was scared.

There were two squash courts at Jacob Hills, one for the officers who were here for the duration of a course and the other for permanently posted officers and their families. I had asked Pam to meet me in the first court, which was in the college premises.

I spotted her at the far end of the room, in a fitted, bright yellow jumpsuit, chatting with some of the other players. I made eye contact with her, pulled a chair and waited for her to come to me.

In less than five minutes, the voluptuous honey bee was buzzing close. Pam was a lovely woman to know in the moments she wasn't so obsessed with herself.

Anyone would have jumped at the offer she had made me, but I had been with my fair share of women over the years, and I figured that most were the same once the paint came off. I had the real thing with Eva, and I wouldn't risk it for anything in the world – almost. Focus, I reminded myself.

Right now I needed Pam to latch on to Maj. Thakur. He usually came in at six. It was fifteen past six now. I asked Pam to point him out to me.

Maj. Thakur wore white shorts, a red T-shirt and white socks pulled up to his knees. He was good-looking in a rugged sort of way, and had short, prickly hair standing on his head. An army cut gone wrong, I thought.

It was his turn to play next and I saw him deliver a rail and a great drive. He had a powerful hand and there were murmurs of a 'nice get'. He showed no mercy for his opponent hitting the ball hard.

He won the game by eleven points and stepped off the court. The waiter served him water, which he declined, and instead picked up a face towel to wipe his face and neck. He then moved outdoors and pulled out a packet of the cheap Charminar cigarettes from his pocket. He was a chain smoker, all right. Only a heavy smoker would choose cigarettes over water after a rough game of squash.

It was then that Santa's little helper, Pam, sneaked up on him and gushed over his game. I watched him smile appreciatively at her, and give her a few pointers on how to hold the racquet just right. It is another matter that Pam was no novice – the credit for her shapely figure went to squash.

He openly flirted with Pam, going on to wonder aloud why he had not had the pleasure of her company before. Pam very cleverly deflected such questions and said, 'My throat is parched and I need a drink,' and simply walked away. He quickly stubbed out his cigarette and followed her to the bar at the terrace. Good dog.

It was past seven and the bar was beginning to fill up. I watched them from the entrance as they ordered their drinks. Pam was very popular, and officers and other ladies came and stopped by to say hello. Maj. Thakur watched all of this with great interest. After Pam had met all and sundry, she settled on a bar stool and began to chat the major up. I took a seat close by and ordered myself a drink, trying my best not to draw attention to myself.

'You are here alone or with family, Major?' Pam began to gently probe into his wife's whereabouts.

'I am due home in twenty days. Sayonara, Jacob Hills!'

'Where is home?'

'Home is where the heart is, Ma'am.'

The clever bastard wasn't going to tell her anything. I stood up and began walking towards Pam, but she warned me with a frosty stare to stay away.

Instead I went to the billiards room to play a game and keep an eye on them. Ten minutes later, Pam came in all huffed and said, 'That man shouldn't be let loose like that.'

'Why?'

'The idiot burnt a hole in my jumpsuit trying to put out his cigarette!'

Dirty habits seldom die. I couldn't keep the triumphant look from appearing on my face.

'Why do you look so happy, Georgy? He's not your man. His wife is pregnant and getting bigger and bigger by the day. That leaves him free to play the field.'

'The bastard said that to you?'

'Not in so many words, but every man is a dog, Georgy – only you are of a different breed, a loyal breed.'

'Pam, sometimes even Gary seems less coarse than you. You get your kicks out of talking dirty, don't you?'

Pam laughed her charming laugh.

'Oh, he also said that his pregnant wife, Anita, is with his parents in Barrackpore.'

Barrackpore was barely twenty-three kilometres from Calcutta, and hadn't Eva heard the dead woman sing in Bengali? I was now certain that this was our man and that there was no pregnant Anita in Barrackpore to find.

All we needed now was for someone to go to Barrackpore, find the truth and the bastard would be caught up in his lies.

'Thanks, Pam, you have been a great help.'

'Thank A.R. for being a sucker for a pretty face.'

'A.R.! You said, A.R.?'

'Yes, his name is Arbind, but his friends call him A.R.'

I almost shouted the name out loud. Of course, he was A.R.! If Gurinder could be Gary and Parminder could be Pam, then Arbind could surely be A.R.!

Anita weds A.R.

The engraving on the pendant made perfect sense.

I got back home and filled Col. Sampat in. He told me he had a course mate who was posted in Fort William, the army establishment in Calcutta, and he would ask him to send a smart chap over to Barrackpore to cross-check right away.

Eva was thrilled at the latest developments, but not about the dressing down Tehlan gave me. She was very apologetic. I assured her it wasn't her fault. She was right to worry, the child needed help. Now we had to figure out why the Tehlans were unwilling to help their own daughter.

Drudgery

Everyone wants to know what happened at the church. I lost control, that's what happened that evening, and the same emotion now returned with full force.

Maj. Alex, who had gotten his men killed. The Charlie who doesn't drink or smoke, who can't get anything right. Even screw a woman right.

I thought of Col. Sampat's pointed questions. The contempt in Mrs Chandy's blue eyes made me angry. To hell with them!

What did they know about me? I looked around my room; everything was kept neatly in its place. I am an organized man who doesn't like a mess. That's why I had gone to the church.

I picked up my stamp collection and stared at it. My father had started it when he was seven. When I was old enough, he passed it on to me.

My old man doted on me and told anyone who cared to listen that his son had the finest collection of stamps in the country. He didn't think less of me even when I told him about the incident in Nagaland.

He was proud of me despite my failures. It was his love that had kept me alive the last few years – the way his eyes lit up when I went back home. He lived with my elder brother and his family.

My niece and nephews were all proud of me, but I have lived this lie long enough. I met them only for fifty days a year; the remaining three hundred and fifteen were a struggle, full of flashbacks, nightmares and sleepless nights.

I had gone to an army doctor immediately after the incident. He had said I could be suffering from Post Traumatic Stress Disorder (PTSD) and that I should get myself admitted. I had heard stories of some really crazy officers locked up in the psych ward of the army hospital after serving in the border areas.

I never went to the hospital again because I was afraid it would hamper my career.

I wasn't suffering from anxiety or a psychological trauma. I was just disturbed. Hell, I had been disturbed for years.

Maybe that had been my mistake – I did need the treatment. Over the years, the problem had only gotten worse. The memories now followed me wherever I went, like ghosts chasing a shadow.

I hid behind my virtuousness and pretended to like the

way my life had turned out. But the sad truth is that I am full of envy. I envy other officers, their carefree laughter and happy families, their lives free of the burden of the dead perched on their shoulder. The cosy dinner parties, where I stand in a corner nursing a soft drink. Sometimes I curse myself for going back to rescue her when I had left her there to die.

Had I stuck to the plan, I wouldn't be staring at these empty walls again. I shouldn't have taken Chandy's wife to the roof knowing fully well that she was there.

It's funny how my conscience was dead all that while. The blood didn't bother me, neither the pain in that voice. All I saw was the drudgery of my own living, reflected in hers. My experience with death is that it comes in its own sweet time and never when you want it to come.

But how long can one wait?

The Frog and the Princess

I was in class when the peon came to tell me that there was a phone call for me in the staffroom. George had never called me at school before. It must be urgent.

I told the children not to make noise and that if anyone was found out of their seats they would have to stand on one leg.

I was becoming stricter with them day by day, the result of which was that the class ran much more smoothly than when I had joined. I was learning that both children and adults needed a firm hand, or they took you for granted.

The phone call had got disconnected by the time I reached the staffroom. I waited for the phone to ring again. It did.

George's voice was calm as he informed me that he had sent a vehicle to bring me home. That had me worried.

'George, please tell me your leg is all right.'

'I am fine, Eva. Just come home.'

'No, first tell me what's wrong? Please.'

'They found Alex's body this morning. He hung himself.'

I felt like I had been hit by a moving truck. I had just met him the day before, rather had insulted and sent him away. I could hear George's voice coming from afar. The receiver fell from my hand. I saw again the hurt look on Alex's face from the previous evening.

'Oh, George, I was wrong, wasn't I?' I picked up the receiver and spoke into it.

'It's all right, Eva, you didn't push him to it.'

I closed my eyes to contain the tears, but there was no holding them back. I had been so caught up with the dead that I never saw that the living weren't really living.

I got home and let George hug me tight and comfort me.

'Eva, they found a letter in his pocket. Colonel Sampat told me about it over the phone.'

Col. Sampat was right about it being too much of a coincidence – three people turning up at the same place, at the same time.

Alex had gone to the church that evening to jump from the highest peak of Jacob Hills and end his life. He had climbed the stairs to the roof, only to find that a woman had already beaten him to it. Anita had been lying there, bleeding. At first he had rushed to help the woman. But she didn't want his help, and had begged him to leave her alone.

He had been surprised that someone who was hurt so

badly didn't want help. But hadn't he gone there to kill himself?

He had tried to reason with her, but she had pushed him away saying, 'Please, I am dying ... let me be.'

The suffering on Anita's face and the pathos in her voice told Alex that she wished for nothing in that moment but an end to her life.

In the last line of the letter, Alex had written that he didn't know what more he could do so he had left her alone.

And then he had met me outside the church.

I had said to him, 'A life can't be snuffed out at the whim of men. All life is His to give or take.'

That's what made Alex turn back to save Anita.

And I, who believed herself to be a good woman, had failed to see the helplessness in his eyes.

Fate had led me to Alex to save him, but I couldn't see past my own paranoia. The night of the party, he had simply wanted to help, but I was tipsy and scared and I had lashed out at him.

Isn't this what we do all the time? We are only interested in other people's lives as long as it amuses or affects us, or helps fulfil our image of ourselves as good human beings, our quota of nobility.

But then again, Alex was just another acquaintance, and whatever problems he may have had weren't my problems, simply because I didn't know they existed.

I wondered how many people lived like that, with issues

and anxieties that were killing them from the inside? What about the reputation Alex had gathered – a man of God?

A man of God wouldn't kill himself.

Brig. Sargam ordered George to take Alex's coffin to his family in Mangalore. The goverment wasn't obliged to pay for flying the body home as it was a suicide. Only the martyrs went home on goverment expense. The brigadier Sargam had been magnanimous and invoked the provision that allowed Jacob Hall to cough up the travelling expenses of the officer travelling with the body.

Alex's father requested that his body be sent home before the rigor mortis set in completely.

The news of Alex's death had a strange effect on Jacob Hills. The climate grew colder. We witnessed the first hailstorm of winter.

The whole station was abuzz with the news. All kinds of stories were being told about why he would have killed himself. People suddenly remembered that he was a 'fine chap'. Everybody claimed to know him well and couldn't believe that Alex would do something like that.

Col. Sampat rang our doorbell as George finished packing his overnight bag. He had come to discuss the information that Alex's letter contained about Anita's death.

Now we knew why Anita didn't give us the name of her attacker at the hospital – she had simply wanted to die.

At first, I found it difficult to come to terms with the fact that a woman was willing to end her life instead of taking steps to change her situation. I told the colonel so.

'Given the circumstances, it was the easiest way out for the poor woman. If it weren't for the missing sandals, I would have believed that Anita had actually stabbed herself,' Col. Sampat said.

'I refuse to believe that!'

The colonel had seen many cases over the course of his career, including some appalling ones.

He told us about the wife of a Lieutenant Colonel, who had taken her children, a boy aged eight and a girl aged twelve, to the kitchen one night and shut all the windows and the door. The children knew something was terribly wrong when their mother poured kerosene all over them. They tried to get away, but she was well prepared for such contingencies and hit the son with a curtain rod. The girl was bigger and stronger and resisted the blows, but the mother gripped the children tightly and, with steady fingers, lit the matchstick. The flames swept upon them instantly, the children struggled in her arms, kicked and pushed, but to no avail, she held on tight.

The cries of the children could be heard a block away. As the fire raged, the mother's grip loosened and the girl slipped from her hold. She managed to roll on the carpet in the living room and douse the flames. The mother and son died on the spot but the daughter was able to crawl out alive. If seventy per cent burns could be called alive.

The indents where the steel rod had hit the child's head were so deep that the doctors were astounded a mother would do this to her own child. The daughter breathed long enough to tell them what happened, but died before her father could return from his posting in J&K.

Soon the story tumbled out that the husband was having an affair with another woman. His wife had killed herself over his infidelity, taking her children with her, because who would look after them when she was gone? It was a senseless act, but to her, it must have made perfect sense. In a similar case, an estranged wife had poisoned her children and herself.

Is there no end to a woman's stupidity, I wondered.

If she really wanted out, why didn't she just take her kids and walk out? Is a woman's life worth giving up for a man's infidelity or his atrocities?

And what about the husband? There are costs on both sides. Was his crime so great that he has to spend the rest of his life with the knowledge that his infidelity cost him the lives that they had created?

Anita didn't have to die. She could have sought help; she chose not to. I felt angry with her for running away from life and letting her husband off the hook so easily.

'Colonel, her husband didn't kill her once, he had been turning the knife in her heart every day of her life with him. We can't let that man get away.'

In response, Col. Sampat gave us another piece of bad

news. Maj. Arbind Thakur's wife was indeed living in Barrackpore with his parents, and was very much pregnant. The chap his course mate had sent over had seen the wife, spoken to the neighbours and local people. Maj. Thakur was the last lead we had on Anita's killer. One A.R. was dead and the other's wife was alive. Then who was Anita's tormentor?

George left the evening before for Mangalore and I was all alone. When he was away, I liked to be close to his things. I went and sat at his desk. I touched his ink pen, the files and his red dairy. As I read what he had written last night, I got all teary-eyed. I love this man, body, heart and soul.

From here we go our separate ways,
I don't think I can walk alone,
Just this night in between,
And the dark hour will be upon our head,
I could fall at your feet,
But surrender happened long ago,
Now the soul yearns to know yours,
In simple things our happiness.

I reread it and put it back. It made me miss him more. He was happy enough, but now more than ever, I found him spending time on his desk, writing. I wished we could get away from this place. I thought of calling Pam but then changed my mind. I had school in the morning and I was not in the mood for frivolous gossip after the events of the last few days.

George would return in two days. Before leaving, he had insisted that we forget about Anita and get back to our lives. I was okay with that, but my mind would keep wondering about Anita's mystery murderer.

Quite a few courses were coming to an end. Once this man left Jacob Hills, it would be as if Anita never existed. My head was beginning to ache – I had to put her out of my mind.

The children were playing in the park. I soaked in the winter sun and checked their answer sheets. I had a little respite, but it didn't last long because Bunny and Junaira got into a fight. I was worried for Junaira. Bunny was a mean fighter – a few boys in the class had lost their milk teeth to her.

Two more kids jumped into the fight, and it became a free for all. Suddenly, the weirdest thing happened. Bunny fell to the ground, clutching something close to her chest and started to cry. Junaira and the other kids stopped in their tracks. No one had ever seen her crying. She was the class bully, she made others cry.

I felt at a loss about what to do. Hesitantly, I picked her up. She didn't resist as I took her back to the classroom. I tried to open her fist, but she wouldn't let go of whatever it was she was holding.

I sat there looking at her wailing. My heart went out to her.

'Bunny, don't cry. Tell me who hurt you, and I'll punish him or her, I promise.'

'You promise?'

She wiped her tears and looked up at my face to gauge if I was really going to come through on my promise. She made up her mind quickly and asked me to punish Junaira, to make her sit like a chicken all day long in the sun. As an afterthought she said that maybe Junaira could be a chicken the next day as well.

I was secretly laughing at the cunning little child, but I kept a serious face and asked, 'Why, what did Junaira do to you, Bunny?'

Bunny opened her fist angrily and threw the piece of paper she had in her fist at me and said, 'She says my papa is like Garba papa!'

I bent down to pick up the chit that had a Garba papa drawing on it and asked, 'And why did she say that?'

'Because her papa doesn't tell her goodnight stories like my papa.'

That still didn't tell me anything. I went in search of Junaira. These children were driving me mad. What possible similarity was there between a yellow, bouncing blob and Col. Tehlan?

'He told the frog and princess story after Bunny's birthday party,' Junaira told me.

'You stayed the night at Bunny's house?'

'I was in Mini's bed and then Bunny's papa told the story of the frog and the princess. He sat like a frog and Bunny had to kiss him and he became a prince.'

'He didn't ask you to kiss him, did he?'

'No, I was sleeping.'

'How can you sleep and listen to the story? You pretended to be asleep. Why?'

'He was very fat and big like Garba papa, and Mamma says its poppy shame to look at people when they are not wearing clothes.'

I couldn't believe my ears. Junaira had seen Bunny's father, the respected Col. Tehlan, stark naked in Bunny's bed?

No, that can't be true ... It was just a child's imagination! Was it? Bunny was being sexually abused and, contrary to what George's psychiatrist friend Rajan had said about disassociation, I think Bunny remembered everything.

What she just didn't know was the difference between right and wrong. I recalled the times that I had seen Col. Tehlan carry her around. A six-year-old child loved to run and play around, but she was always in his lap. She adored him. Now I knew why she wouldn't tell anyone who had hurt her. It must seem like a game to her. A game her father played with her while telling her fairytales like the frog and the princess, his own dirty versions of them.

Was I jumping to conclusions? What the hell was the

matter with me? I couldn't just sit here and talk to myself. I decided to go meet Wilhelmina before taking any drastic steps.

I walked up to the hospital. Wilhelmina was on her rounds with the doctor in one of the wards.

She saw me and smiled, 'Give me five minutes; I am done here.'

I was restless and began pacing the lobby.

'What's with you, Eva, got ants in your pants?' She laughed, coming out with a tray in her hand. I charged at her.

'Wilhelmina, can a father sexually abuse his own daughter?'

'Of course, honey, he's got the equipment.'

She saw the look on my face and said, 'Mostly people don't talk about it, but incest, sure as hell, happens. Father, brother, uncle, you name it, all fucking bastards.'

'What about the mother, you think she knows and does not do anything about it?'

'It's not normal, but there have been cases where the mother knows about the abuse and doesn't lift a finger. It could be due to economic reasons, like financial support, or ... a more twisted one, like feeling threatened that the girl child has the father's attention.'

'That would mean that the mother, instead of holding the father responsible, would blame the daughter for the abuse?'

'Are we talking about Bunny here? Her parents fit the pattern: they never came back, there was no concern for her safety and not once did they ask about the long-term effect of the trauma on the child. And they are educated – at least the father seems to be. That tells you a lot about the family.'

I told her about Junaira's Garba papa.

'Goodness gracious me! Jacob Hills has become a regular Peyton Place!'

'What's that?'

'Honey, you should read more. It's a novel, but it is based on true accounts of real people with sordid secrets in small towns in America. You have incest, abortion, adultery and murder all in one place. There is Selena, the sixteen-year-old girl who kills and buries her stepfather under a sheep pen after being sexually abused for years. But that story is based on the life of a real girl who murdered her own abusive father. Grace Metalious wrote the book in 1956 and, hey, we live in the eighties.'

'I don't think Bunny is going to be killing her father anytime soon. Hell, she doesn't even realize it's wrong! By the time it hits her, her psyche would be completely damaged. We have to do something.'

'Can you repeat this in front of Col. Verma? He's the head of the Military Hospital, and he can take it up with the right people. He's a good man.'

Wilhelmina picked up Bunny's report and requested the

doctor on duty to come along and we went to meet Col. Verma.

He was initially sceptical about the Garba papa story, but when he read the doctor's remark on Bunny's report, his face hardened.

'The girl child shows no sign of fear or discomfort at the vaginal examination, and seems rather used to being probed and prodded.'

I Want My Money Back

There was still time before college term, but I knew I wanted to study Sociology and Gender Studies. I no longer wished to further my husband's career. I didn't love this man and he had never, for an instant in our marriage, shown me that he was human.

Now the rules were about to change. I was going to get an education, and he was going to pay for it. And if he so much as raised his voice at me, I would send a written complaint to the army chief and his career would be as good as over.

I didn't just sleep with those men; I listened and I learnt. A wife has a lot of rights in the army. I only had to raise my voice against the mental and physical harassment he had put me through, and Vikram would probably go home a superseded major.

Yes, I had learnt that this huge organization had all its systems in place. Those who flouted its rules could only do so as long as no one knew what they were up to. All that happened behind closed doors remained behind closed doors. People weren't important, but the system was, and none of it could ever be allowed to come out. If I decided to bring things out into the open, the same men who ganged up with Vikram to make me what I have become would then throw him to the wolves.

Now I saw the Key Club clearly – they were just a handful of bored and depraved men and women who brought shame to the name of the very organization that lent them class and dignity. And wannabes like Vikram and I were so influenced by our social inadequacy that we wanted to emulate them.

After that night, I chanced upon Gary frequently at parties, and he treated me as he behaved with all the other ladies, with utmost respect. Not a word nor a hint of what had or had not happened between us that night.

Pam spoke to me as casually as ever, nothing in her manner suggested that her husband had spent a night sprawled in my living room. There was no tenderness or attachment – the experiment lasted only for one night.

The other couples also moved around laughing, making polite conversation. Life was the same for everyone, except me.

Today, I would show him the admission form for the Girls' College. The fee was not much, especially for a man who had received thousands of rupees in cash and a piece of land worth lakhs in dowry.

I sat at the dining table looking at the admission form. It was complete, except for the demand draft of five hundred rupees and Vikram's signature as my guardian.

I heard his Bullet in the drive ... That had also been bought with my father's money.

'Why is the front door open, and where is my lunch? I have to get back in half an hour.' He walked in, dumped his briefcase on the sofa and looked at the dining table in surprise.

'Lunch is ready, Vikram. I want you to look at this.'

I gave the form to him.

'Have you gone mad? People here don't know that you have only studied till high school, but if you start going to college they will find out that I married an illiterate woman from the village.'

'What's wrong with that, Vikram? You are also from the same village. And I am not asking for your permission, I am going to college. I want you to give me a thousand rupees.'

'Get lost! I am not giving you my money!'

'Fine, give it to me out of my father's money.'

'Bitch! Your father's money has all gone in feeding, clothing and transforming you – a social embarrassment – into a high-class woman.'

'A high-class woman you could pimp to get you a promotion?'

He slapped me so hard I fell off the chair and my face hit the cold floor.

I ran my tongue inside my mouth and tasted blood. Two

of my front teeth had come out. I stared at them in horror and couldn't control the shaking that took over my body. I was nothing much to look at, and now I had crossed over to ugly.

'Serves you right! Never speak to me like that ever again, or I'll break the rest of them too.'

He went into the kitchen, helped himself to the dal-chawal I had made for lunch, and sat down to eat on the sofa. I lay there crying, while he ate his lunch as if nothing had happened. The rays of the sun fell into the living room and onto his head. From where I lay, he looked like any other man.

I imagined just for a minute what life would have been like if we had been a regular couple. He would have come home and hugged me. We would have sat down to eat, and discussed the small, irrelevant happenings of the day, laughing occasionally.

He belched and walked past me with a kick in my direction. No, he wasn't like other men. He had no heart.

'Are you going to lie here the whole day? The batman will be coming soon. Get up and fix yourself.'

With that he picked up his briefcase and went out.

I picked myself up from the floor, the broken teeth tightly clutched in my hand and went to the bathroom. I rinsed my mouth with water and saw the blood mix with it. I stood there a long time, still not looking at the mirror.

And when I did, I cried some more. The image of my tear stained, toothless face shook me up. Is this how I was going to spend my life, with this animal breaking me bit by bit, inch by inch?

I picked up the phone and dialled a number.

'Hello.'

'Hello, this is Saryu. Will you help me send a letter to the army chief?'

'You can't be serious, Saryu. It'll ruin him.'

'Trust me, he deserves it.'

I put the receiver down and went to his study. I took out four plain sheets of paper and began to write my story from the very beginning.

I knew the dates, names and personal identification numbers of the men Vikram had sent me to. I didn't have much of a vocabulary, but I had a great memory and I used it to piece together my story.

I wrote and rewrote, tossing paper in the waste basket till it was full. The complexes of inadequacy and inequity ran so deep that, even at a time like this, I was more concerned about the grammar and the spellings. I didn't want be dismissed as an uneducated woman who had the good fortune of marrying an army officer.

I felt ashamed as I wrote about my part in it, thinking how strange men in olive uniforms would read and review it. I had done what I had done. If I expected Vikram to take responsibility for it, I must do the same. I may not know how to spell words, but I had feelings. And it's with that pent-up rage that I wrote and kept writing till the ink in the pen ran out.

George

A Jolly Good Fellow

It had been a long and emotionally exhausting trip. Alex's father had collapsed right in front of my eyes as he saw the coffin. His older son, Mathew, and I picked him up, but he was unable to walk. We had carried him to the bed and watched the old man shed tears of grief.

I had never seen a man cry like a child. It was a sight that chilled my heart. All I could do was curse Alex for putting his father through this. The truth is, everyone is dispensable in this world. Life goes on for the wife, lover, children and siblings. Maybe painfully, but it goes on nevertheless.

But parents can never learn to deal with the loss of his child. The memories of the child learning to walk, talk, go to school, haunt them for all time. They spend their lives chasing after their children, to give them a good life. They share in their children's victories and defeats. And in Alex's case, he did not die in a war or an accident – he took his own life. It must have been terribly painful for his father to think his child was in so much pain and he did not know of it till now, when it was too late to do anything.

Alex couldn't move past that one mistake and drowned in his own guilt.

It seems the wheel of guilt is never-ending. It keeps rolling and destroys all the goodness that you have in you.

Back home, I reached for the Tiger balm – the vein in my temple was throbbing and an ugly headache had come on. Eva was sound asleep, her mouth slightly open.

She breathed through her mouth when she slept. I had tried to get her to breathe through the nose, but after some time, she would lapse into her old habit. I kissed her hair lightly.

She had been through much in my absence. She had to repeat Bunny's story many times and with much conviction before the matter was taken further.

No one was willing to believe that a respected man, a father, would do something like this to his own daughter. She had been ridiculed and accused of slandering the reputation of an officer, but she had held her ground.

The commandant had been furious that such a scandal was brewing under his nose, and had finally ordered an inquiry. But Col. Tehlan was not one to give up easily. He threatened to expose the commandant's affairs with his maid. Gary told me some kind of a deal was struck; 'you watch my back and I'll watch yours', and Col. Tehlan's posting orders had come a day later.

The bastard sent his wife and kids to Ambala, his home town, on the first train out of Jacob Hills, so that no one got a chance to question his daughter. Despite all our efforts, Col. Tehlan's punishment was that he was going to a new place, to start afresh.

I got out of bed to make us tea. It was six; time to wake her up. Gary and Pam had invited us for dinner at the club. I wasn't very keen on going, but it was their sixth anniversary, and Eva, my babe in the woods, thought it would be really mean of us not to join them in their anniversary celebration. Six years of love, joy and infidelity! Hell, we couldn't miss that!

We were at the club sharp at eight, but the hosts hadn't turned up. It had to be Pam's doing. I am sure she was dressing to kill and dear Gary must be amusing himself with a drink at home.

No harm done. I was happy to spend some quiet time with my usually not-so-quiet wife. Eva was wearing a dark blue silk sari, a shade darker than her eyes and looked beautiful. I could just look at her. She asked me to stop staring and find us a table.

I chose a table in the corner and asked the waiter to get us red wine. The bar was crowded as usual, but the sitting area was quieter, much to Eva's relief.

As soon as she said that, I saw Capt. Rana walking towards us. He wished us both and I offered him a seat, but he refused and just stood there, all hesitant and shy. There was an awkward pause, which Eva filled very skilfully by asking about his wife.

I thought I'd see a grimace, but I saw a wide smile instead and he replied, 'She's sitting over there. I'll just go and get her.'

'No, no, please. I'll go and say hello to her,' Eva said.

Eva got up and walked to where Heena was sipping her lime juice. She looked happily plump.

I offered Rana a cigarette, but he refused.

'No cigarettes?'

'I quit, sir. It's not good for the baby.'

I could only smile and pat him on the back. The joy of seeing the lost come home is always overwhelming.

'Rana, it's the wisest fucking thing that you have ever done in your life.' We both knew I wasn't referring to the smoking.

Eva came back saying what a healthy glow Heena had, and that all she spoke about was how well her husband was looking after her. Rana left a few minutes later, and I knew what was coming next.

'George, I was thinking, maybe we should ...'

'No, we are not talking babies right now, though I don't mind the activity that precedes it.'

Eva rolled her eyes.

Suddenly, there was a tinkling of glasses at the bar. Fifteen-twenty officers grouped around the bar and hoisted a chair in the air and sang, '*For he's a jolly good fellow, and so say all of us*'. A drunk and beaming Col. Tehlan sat on it.

Both Eva and I laughed mirthlessly at the falsity of it all. If these officers knew how jolly good a fellow Tehlan really was, they would probably throw him off the terrace.

The noise continued and they took him around the place, saying, 'Hip, hip, hurray'.

The chair was finally put down, and a swaying, staggering Col. Tehlan thanked everyone and gave a speech about how kind it was of everyone to give him a little impromptu farewell.

'My posting order came very unexpectedly; good soldiers are needed everywhere,' he finished his speech.

I wanted to tell him to shut up, but that would amount to insubordination. I was here with Eva and decided to ignore him. Though looking at Eva's small face, I could tell that she was upset. The man was the lowest creep alive.

I looked at the watch, it was eight-thirty and there was still no sign of Gary and Pam. I snapped my fingers to call the waiter, but he didn't see us. I was looking around for another waiter when my eyes locked with Tehlan's. Damn!

He started advancing towards our table, the bastard. Before I could warn Eva, he was already upon us.

'Mrs Chandy, compliments to you for cooking up stories that beat the imagination of even first graders.'

Eva was angry, but she didn't say anything. He was reeking of liquor.

'Colonel, please leave,' I said to him, trying to retain my cool.

'No, I don't want to make a scene here, either. I just want to ask your wife what's wrong with a father kissing his daughter? Did your father never kiss you, huh? Didn't he tell you bedtime stories?'

He was now bending over her and hissing over her shoulder. We had attracted a bit of attention, I totally detested that.

'Colonel Tehlan, this is the last time I am going to ask you to leave,' I said, my voice firm.

Eva was alarmed at my tone, and signalled that we should leave right away.

Col. Tehlan looked from her to me and said, 'You want to mess up little kids' heads, screw with your own.'

I punched him in the face, really hard. First his glass hit the ground with a thud then his body. Every eye on the terrace was on us now. I took Eva's arm and we started to walk out.

'You son-of-a-bitch, you're not going anywhere!'

Col. Tehlan caught hold of my ankle and yanked with all his might. My leg gave in and pain shot through it like high-voltage current. I almost blacked out and fell hard. I heard Eva's frightened voice call my name and sensed that other officers had surrounded us.

Someone helped the colonel to his feet. He got up wiping his bleeding nose and said jovially, 'Nothing to worry about, boys. Just settling some old score.'

The smug look on the bastard's face got me really mad.

'The colonel's absolutely right, boys. I was just expressing my disgust at him for having fun with his six-year-old daughter. I believe it's called child abuse. Isn't it, Colonel?'

There was a collective intake of breath and all eyes were on Col. Tehlan. His face frozen, he looked like his heart might stop beating. Then he shrugged, pushed through the crowd and walked away with his tail between his legs.

The bastard may have run away, but the thing about the army was that, despite the numbers, it was a small world. There was no escaping the rumour mills – the wives would talk, and the officers sure as hell would recount the story over drinks. For once, I was happy that the grim machinery had its upside too.

'Sir, that can't be true? Did the colonel really ...' Rana's voice carried the disbelief of all present.

'Sorry to disappoint you, folks, but that *is* the disgusting truth.'

There were murmurs of 'the sick motherfucker', but I couldn't care less. My leg that was healing so well was broken again.

Rana came to lend me a hand, but Eva shook her head. She knew that if I could, I would have been up by now.

'We'll have to call for an ambulance,' she said to Rana.

Now, this is what a man like Gary can never understand. A woman who loves you can read the helplessness in your eyes and still think of you as the bravest man in the world. And this I can say with confidence: not every woman can read a man, only the one who owns his soul.

A few officers lifted me and put me on a three-seater sofa. I thanked everyone and shooed them away. 'I am all right now, please carry on.'

Rana went to make the call and Eva went to fetch a glass of whisky from the bar. I badly needed one, the pain was unbelievably cutting.

She came back a little rattled, but I was in so much pain that I snatched the glass from her hand and emptied it in one gulp.

'The third man on the right, close cropped hair; do you know who he is?' Eva asked me out of the blue.

It was Maj. Thakur. 'He said something to you?'

'Not to me, but he was drinking and philosophizing about "the unknown bird in the cage, how does it fly in and out".'

'Ah, well,' I said, holding back the pain, 'all officers are great philosophers after a few drinks.'

There were beads of sweat breaking out on Eva's forehead.

'George, that's the literal translation of what Anita said to me just before she died.'

'I checked. He has a pregnant wife, Eva.'

'No. He *had* one.'

Ashapurna

We were back in Calcutta. George had to be flown out of Jacob Hills for an emergency surgery. The operation went well, but the doctors were not ready to discharge him just yet.

We had been here a week, and most of that time I had spent in the hospital. Things were a little better now, so my mother insisted that I take it easy or they would have to admit me as well. George had given strict orders that I was not to visit the hospital for the next two days.

It was strange: while my parents went to see him at the hospital in the evening, I had to sit at home because my obstinate husband wanted me to get some rest. He was right in a way; I did feel exhausted from all the drama in our lives since we started living in Jacob Hills.

Gary and Pam had called every day to find out how George was doing, and had even offered to come down.

They were good people, a little different in their outlook

towards life, but if everyone were to be like everybody else, the sheer monotony of life would just kill us all.

I had also called Col. Sampat. He was out of office then, but called me back on the number I had left with his PA. He was happy to tell me that a lot of muck from under the carpet was surfacing and he had been busy cleaning up.

He had just come back after taking into custody an officer who apparently pushed his wife to sleep with senior officers.

Wilhelmina had been right in a way. Jacob Hills was indeed the Peyton Place of the eighties. I had just started reading the novel.

I asked him if he could give me the address of Maj. Thakur's wife in Barrackpore.

'You are barking up the wrong tree, Ma'am,' he said.

I set out the next morning for Barrackpore. I told my father I was visiting an old school friend, and that he need not speak of my visit to George. He has kept all my secrets over the years, from my schooldays onwards.

I asked our driver, Kishen, who had been with us for years, to take out the car.

It was a cloudy sky and the sun seemed too lazy to follow us. We left behind the traffic and the teeming slums of the city. I breathed more easily as we moved past the open fields.

I had hoped to spend the journey looking out of the window, but I dozed off.

The journey was short. Barrackpore was only twenty-three kilometres from Calcutta. The road we had taken led us to a bank of the Hooghly river. It seemed like an industrial area. Kishen told me that the first British barrack or cantonment was built here in 1772, and that gave the town its name.

We stopped a couple of times to ask the way. Finally, Kishen stopped the car in front of a dilapidated two-storey building. There were seven or eight young children playing with marbles and three middle-aged women drying fish and spices in the sun and doing some odd jobs. I assumed that theirs was a joint family, and a large one.

The kids stopped playing when I knocked at the door and laughed at me, making fun of my bell-bottoms in Bengali.

I approached the women and told them that I had come to see Arbind's wife. At the mention of Arbind's wife, they became a little wary of me and asked me to come back in the evening when his father was back.

He worked in the jute mill and would be home by five-thirty. I tried again and said that Arbind had sent a gift for his wife. I held out a package that Mamma had given me – a box of foreign chocolates that had come for Durga Puja from one of Papa's friends.

Seeing the brightly wrapped package, they whispered among themselves. One woman led me upstairs through a dingy, dimly lit staircase past small rooms to an even smaller one. A young girl, not be more than fifteen, I was sure, was lying on the bed.

A khes or shawl covered her swollen stomach. Her big, beautiful eyes fringed with black kohl stared into my blue ones.

Her hair was parted in the middle and red sindoor was laid thickly in the partition. She covered her head with the pallu of her purple tant sari, which looked good with the green blouse with puffed sleeves that she was wearing.

Her attire was mismatched, but she looked lovely and her hands were full of colourful bangles.

This was a different world. I didn't know what I had expected when I came here, but I had definitely not expected to see an underage pregnant girl.

I sat down and the other women stood right there, keeping guard.

I gave her the package and said that her husband had sent it. She seemed happy and opened the wrapping immediately.

'How is the baby?' I asked in Bengali.

She said it kicked and kicked, and wouldn't let her sleep. She asked me when her husband was going to come.

A strange question from a wife about her husband, but it told me that he didn't write to her or call her, or perhaps even know anything about her other than what he may have seen of her petite body in this poorly lit room. I was sure she had never been anywhere outside her village. She couldn't have been staying in the SF accommodation in Kanpur.

The older woman was getting impatient and kept looking at the door. I had just one more question to ask, and then I was done here.

'Tomar naam ki?' (What is your name?)

'Ashapurna.'

I repeated her name and thanked her. I held her hand and wished her luck. She made an attempt to get out of bed, but I stopped her, and there in the valley between her breasts, was a fading cigarette burn.

Ashapurna had taken Anita's place.

She was going to give the Thakur household a boy to carry their line forward, something that the first wife could not do.

Thakur had killed Anita because she was no longer needed.

Armed with Ashapurna's name and my impression of her, I went to the hospital to see George and told him everything. We called up Col. Sampat.

Col. Sampat was still not convinced and broke into Maj. Thakur's room while he attended his lectures. He found the silver pendant in the pocket of one of his trousers – probably the pair he had worn to the Husbands' Night.

On finding the pendant, the colonel took personal leave from office and travelled to Kanpur with pictures of Anita. He showed them to the neighbours, who confirmed her to be Maj. Thakur's wife, a timid, unfriendly woman who didn't socialize much.

Now the next and the most crucial step was to find out where Maj. Thakur had been keeping Anita in Jacob Hills. After three days he found the officer who had rented out his house to Thakur for two months.

Anita had come to Jacob Hills in the last week of September and, two weeks later, she had died.

Col. Sampat also found dark stains on a carpet in the officer's living room that had been scrubbed and cleaned, leaving the carpet faded in places. The officer informed him that Thakur had been apologetic about dropping a glass of wine on it.

Once we had this information, George's father called up people at the Army Headquarters in Delhi. A complaint was filed against Thakur and a court of inquiry ordered.

Maj. Thakur, under duress, confessed to having remarried because his first wife was unable to give him a son. He had met Anita four years ago when he was posted in Jammu and they had fallen in love.

Her parents and two brothers were against the inter-caste marriage and she had eloped with him.

Anita belonged to a staunch and affluent Brahmin family. They severed ties with her after she ran away from home, and would have probably killed her if they knew where she was.

They had married and she had moved around with him on his postings.

After three years of trying for a child, Thakur's father

had pressured him into marrying a girl from their own caste. Thakur had gone to Barrackpore on leave seven months ago, and married Ashapurna. Of the ten days he spent in the village, most were spent trying to impregnate the new bride.

Thakur was repentant, but he claimed not to have killed his wife. He was angry with her for writing an anonymous letter to the Army Headquarters about an officer burning little girls with his cigarette.

He had read the circular on the notice board of Jacob Hall and knew it had to be his wife's doing. He had come home wanting to punish her and had told her about Ashapurna and the baby, knowing full well that Anita would put up with anything. She had no place to go.

Anita knew it too and had threatened Thakur that he had to leave the other woman or she would kill herself.

Thakur had laughed and asked her to go ahead; he didn't care.

He was shocked when Anita stabbed herself with the kitchen knife and lay on the carpet in the living room. She was losing blood fast, but he dared not take her to the hospital. They would want to know about the marks on her body.

He waited for her to die. Afternoon turned into evening and she became unconscious. He wondered what to do with her body.

He remembered the story about the old church. He

knew of the leopard's den there and was certain that if she were left there, she would be eaten by an animal. No one came to the abandoned place and Anita was too feeble to scream for help. He could have killed her, but he couldn't bring himself to kill her in cold blood.

Finally, he had put her in the car on the back seat over plastic sheets and old newspapers and carried her to the roof of the church.

As he lay her down on the terrace, she regained consciousness. Her eyes followed his every movement and he couldn't bear the look in her eyes any longer and had left her there, sure that by nightfall she would be dead.

He admitted that her family wasn't likely to come, so he assumed that no one would miss her.

Thakur glibly told the officers heading the inquiry that he had panicked, thinking the police wouldn't believe him if he said Anita had tried to kill herself, and it was this fear that had made him leave her at the church.

But that still didn't explain the ugly burn marks on her breasts, around her navel and inside of her thighs. The autopsy report had confirmed physical abuse over a long period of time.

No amount of skilful storytelling could get Maj. Thakur off the hook. It also came to the army's notice that, in his previous posting, he had been banned from several homes when girls had complained to their mothers about Thakur Uncle putting his tongue in their mouths. After obtaining the testimony of witnesses both civilian and official for a month, the summary of evidence was recorded.

Thakur was court-martialled and, though the army punishes its own, in this case there was double jurisdiction – Thakur marrying a minor made it a rape case.

He was handed over to the police and was being tried in criminal court for raping a minor, mentally and physically torturing his wife and abetting her suicide.

He was looking at a prison term of no less than fourteen years. I wished they would just hang him.

The only tragedy in all of this was that of Ashapurna. Her big eyes in her small face haunted my sleep. She always asked the same question, 'When is my husband going to come home?'

The War Is On

The bell rang at eight in the morning. I saw them through the keyhole: four men in uniform. I was afraid; perhaps they had come for me. Maybe Vikram had manipulated them into believing that I was mad and needed to be locked away for good.

I opened the door and stared at the big man who stood in front wearing a pleasant smile.

He introduced himself as Col. Sampat and assured me that they were here for my husband.

Vikram was in uniform, ready to leave for office and was surprised to see the Military Police at his doorstep – the striking red berets, the guns and an envelope that bore his name.

He took the letter, read through it and said, not in the least disturbed, 'She's lying.'

'It has come from the top; a court of inquiry has been ordered and you have to be detained till further orders. I suggest you come with us quietly, no point in unnecessarily handcuffing you.'

He gave me a venomous look and requested the colonel to give him two minutes alone with me.

'I'm afraid I can't do that. The letter clearly states that you are not to be left alone with your wife.'

'Why? She's my wife!'

Vikram was puzzled, but I knew what the colonel was talking about. I had written in the letter that I feared for my life.

The pictures of my bruised face, broken teeth and swollen eye must have authenticated the claim, for they had rung the doorbell exactly a day after receiving the letter.

'You slut! After all that I have done for you!' he screamed, and the men pinned him against the wall to handcuff him.

'Vikram, I want to see you stripped of the rank that you are so proud of. I want to see that shame in your eyes that I felt warming the beds of the men you pushed me to.'

'Bitch, you could have said no! I didn't fucking force you to suck cocks! Let's see what people have to say when they hear that!'

I saw Col. Sampat's expression change from sympathy to distaste.

Yes, it was going to get ugly. Under the uniform, they were all naked, a promiscuous man was a Casanova, but a loose woman was a whore.

'No, Vikram you didn't force me, you just manipulated me into believing that if I had to fit in, I had to be like you – kiss ass and suck cocks.'

Epilogue

Heena gave birth to a beautiful baby girl. The father was ecstatic. He spent his entire month's salary and took an overdraft to throw a daru party for the entire course.

Saryu passed out from college with a distinction and went on to do her PhD in Women's Rights. The disappointment of a failed marriage did not stop her from marrying again, and this time for love. Vikram was court-martialled and sent home in disgrace without pension. He was also made to pay compensation over and above the dowry he had received from Saryu's parents. Back in Patna, his parents were able to find him another match from a wealthy family, saying that their son divorced his first wife because she was characterless.

Col. Tehlan was posted near the Burma border. His fellow officers and subordinates despised him, having heard of his infamy. He was left alone to brood in his tent and drink.

Brig. Sargam bought a house in Shimla after retiring as the commandant of Jacob Hills. His wife, the football, continued with her cards and kitty parties, and the brigadier kept busy with golf and the maids as before.

George put in his papers, against his father's wishes, and was discharged from the army. His leg never did heal completely. He settled with Eva in Cochin, grew mushrooms and became a pioneer in mushroom farming in his town. In his free time, he wrote songs and even managed to sell a few to the Malayalam film industry.

Eva joined the Little Angels convent as a teacher and taught English to primary school students. She was happy to have Pam, Gary and their son Goldy spend a week-long holiday on their farm. Gary, on account of his and Pam's accomplishments, continued to serve at Jacob Hall. He was now a senior instructor with the Tactical Wing.

Captain Rana turned out to be a great father and a loving husband. Now, whenever he met a beautiful woman, he looked at her feet instead of her face (well, almost always!).

Bunny grew up to be a beautiful but troubled girl. She graduated in Home Science and English Literature with a third division. The Tehlans were quick to marry her off to an unsuspecting groom from their hometown. Sadly, her marriage was annulled within a month. The bridegroom claimed that his new bride suffered from some kind of psychological disorder. She expected him to read her a story from her fairytale collection every night before they went to bed.

Acknowledgements

When my first *Love on the Rocks* came out in 2011, I arrogantly believed that it was a year-and-a-half's perseverance on my part that finally got the book published. Two years later, I think differently. If it weren't for the love and support of some truly wonderful people I would have never made it this far.

I am very grateful to my mother, Rita Tandon, for shielding me like a rock from the hail falling from the sky; for teaching me the value of compassion to both humans and animals. Without you I am nothing, Mamma.

Thank you, Grandpa, V. M. Tandon, for being a living example of integrity and humility.

I thank my aunt, Neelam Dhankher, for showing me what a magical, spiritual journey life is. For being an epitome of unconditional love, strength, grace and a guiding light.

My story, my characters would be quite lacklustre if it weren't for the insightful character illustrations drawn by my talented sister-in-law, Pavitra S. Tandon. Her passion for her work and for my brother is a great inspiration. My brother, Om Tandon, is a visionary. I would like to quote him here, 'Everyone can make money; we are here to make a name'. Thank you for encouraging me to dream through all the confusion and chaos.

A heartfelt thank you to my lifeline – Retd. Lt. General

Rameshwar Roy and Luxmi Roy for opening the doors to the world of meditation for me. It's a great blessing to have someone so learned and so wise by my side. Thank you for reminding me that I am a mighty river.

To my aunt, Priti Quinn, for being a storehouse of stories and a powerhouse of love, warmth and affection. For flying halfway across the world to pay her last respects to my father.

To the brilliant Dr Neha Prakash for opening her heart and her home to me when I needed it most. Thank you for helping me stand on my feet. To Swati Vashishtha, journalist, ace photographer and a fellow Sufi Masroof for her encouraging words.

To my editor, Ajitha G. S., for believing in my writing and for saying all the wonderful things that writers long to hear from their editors. Your thoughtfulness and patience gave me the confidence to finish my third and fourth book.

To Natasha Puri for being so gracious while editing *Jacob Hills*. Thank you for making my book read even better.

To Vaishali Mathur for boosting my self-confidence when I was at a loss for what to do next.

To my literary agent, Kanishka Gupta, for bringing my dream to be an author to life.

To Om Swami, my friend, guide and spiritual Guru, thank you for loving me. In you I see whom I wish to be.

To Praneet Dhankher, the finest and the most generous

man I know and admire. Thank you for standing by me in all my good–bad decisions, for being happy for me even at the cost of your own happiness. You are sealed like a flower; a flower I treasure, a flower buried deep in my heart, forever.

Finally, to George for being George.